CITY OF DEATH

CITY OF DEATH

TONY SQUIRE

CONTENTS

Dedication   vii

1 CITY OF SHADOWS   1

2 FAMILY TIES   17

3 A STICKY SITUATION   31

4 DON'T LOOK NOW   46

5 THE ANDES AWAIT   64

6 GODS OF FIRE   81

7 JUSTICE   101

8 EVERY SHADOW A SUSPECT   118

9 STRENGTH IN NUMBERS   137

10 AN UNWANTED PRESENCE   152

11 THE GIFT   170

12 DANGER CLOSE   196

13 HERE WE GO AGAIN!   214

14 TO THE FUTURE AND BEYOND   229

About the Author   **241**
More Books By This Author   **242**

For my beautiful wife Sheila.

CHAPTER 1

CITY OF SHADOWS

The Andes, 1533

The jungle breathed around them - humid, thick with the stench of decay. Somewhere in the distance, something growled, a jaguar maybe, its warning lost beneath the crack of branches as the Spanish soldiers pushed forward, hacking through the undergrowth with their swords. They had been marching for days, their rations low, their patience thinner than their rusting chain-mail.

Leading them was Capitan Hernando Ortega, a veteran of Pizarro's conquest, his breastplate dulled by the sweat of the jungle, his helmet dented from countless skirmishes. His men - twenty hardened conquistadors - dragged themselves forward, their boots sinking into the mud. Beside them, Brother Diego, a Dominican friar, clutched a leather-bound book to his chest, whispering prayers between ragged breaths.

Then they saw it.

The jungle parted like a curtain, revealing a city older than the Incas, its stone walls covered in intricate carvings depicting figures that did not look human. Towering golden spires gleamed in the last light of the setting sun, their surfaces untouched by time or war.

And at the heart of it all, inside a temple crowned with a massive obsidian dome, sat the treasure they had come for – mountains of gold, piled high like an offering to forgotten gods.

But there was something else...something more.

Beneath the golden hoard, half-buried by time and neglect, were great wheels of metal, strange tubes, and crystalline structures that shimmered with a light of their own. Not gold, not jewels, but something unnatural - a construction that did not belong in this world.

The Spaniards hesitated. This was no mere temple of a heathen people. This was something older; something untouched by time.

Ortega stepped forward, his breath catching in his throat. Along the walls and high on the vaulted ceilings, vessels of smooth glass radiated light. They were not candles, not flames, but something different – a steady, unnatural glow that did not flicker or waiver. His men whispered prayers, crossing themselves, for this was no work of God.

"What sorcery is this?" one of them muttered.

Ortega's gaze fell upon the massive circular device near the far wall, half-hidden beneath the gold. Wheels within wheels. Great arcs of metal, intricate carvings of unknown symbols. He stepped closer, his fingers itching to touch its surface. It was warm and seemed to be the source of power which operated the strange lights. But the machine itself had no power source, its massive wheels turning kinetically as if alive.

Then it began to hum.

Low and deep, it vibrated through the stone floor, rattling the very air around them. The soldiers shifted uneasily, their swords and arquebuses at the ready.

"Madre de Dios...!" Ortega breathed, awe tightening his grip on his sword.

Behind him, his men murmured in disbelief. Gold. Enough to buy kingdoms. Enough to make emperors kneel. But what was this strange device that stood before them?

Brother Diego fell to his knees, crossing himself.

"We must not touch it. It is not of this world and is not ours to take".

Ortega ignored him. He raised his sword.

"This city belongs to Spain. Take what you can carry!"

The soldiers surged forward.

And the jungle screamed.

From the shadows of the ruins, they came. Silent, unseen, death incarnate.

The first man died before he could even cry out. A spear, carved from black obsidian, punched through his throat, spraying hot blood over the gold. His body convulsed, choking on crimson, before vanishing into the undergrowth.

Then, the war horns sounded.

The air filled with whistling projectiles – flint tipped arrows, poison darts, jagged throwing axes.

A second soldier stumbled, clutching his face as a barbed dart pierced his eye, sinking deep into his skull. He slumped to the ground, his body jerking, twitching.

"A las armas! To arms!" Ortega roared.

But the enemy was already among them.

From the temple shadows emerged warriors covered in black body paint, their skin glistening, their eyes glowing in the firelight. They wielded clubs lined with razor sharp volcanic glass, their movements inhumanly fast.

A Spaniard swung his sword, but before the blade could land, a warrior side stepped and slammed a macauhuitl - a wooden sword with several embedded obsidian blades - into his skull. The bone split open like a ripe fruit, brains and blood splattering across the gold.

Another soldier tried to reload his musket, but a jaguar cloaked warrior tackled him, driving a sharp knife deep into his stomach. The Spaniard screamed as his intestines spilled onto the temple floor, steam rising from his open belly.

Brother Diego ran for the altar, clutching his cross.

"Dios nos protégé! God protect us!"

An arrow punctured his throat. He gurgled, sinking to his knees, blood bubbling from his mouth. His book, now stained red, slipped from his hands.

Ortega swung wildly, his sword slicing through flesh, but it wasn't enough. He turned, searching for his men – only to see them drowning in a sea of black clad warriors, hacked to pieces.

The jungle floor turned to mud, soaked with Spanish blood.

Then came the beast.

From the temple steps, a massive figure loomed – seven feet tall, wearing a mask fashioned from a jaguar's skull. He held a staff crowned with a glowing blue crystal.

Ortega barely had time to take in what he was seeing before the crystal flared, sending a wave of energy through the battlefield.

His men convulsed, screaming, as their bodies crumpled. Their weapons turning to dust in their hands.

Ortega fell to his knees, his sword slipping from his grip.

The last thing he saw was the masked warrior towering over him, wielding a huge bloodstained glass sword.

Then - darkness.

The temple burned, the fire ignited by fallen torches which the soldiers had carried. The warriors dragged the Spanish corpses into the flames, their bodies crackling, their screams swallowed by the roar of the inferno. The air stank of blood and burnt flesh, the jungle itself seeming to exhale in satisfaction.

But one man escaped.

Brother Diego, bleeding, broken, but alive.

He stumbled into the tangled undergrowth, barely able to breathe. His ribs ached where he'd been struck, his robes soaked with his own blood. But in his trembling hands, clutched to his chest like the Holy Grail itself, was his book - his only salvation, the only record of the expedition. As he crawled through the jungle he whispered the only words he could still form.

"Dios...perdoname..."

A secret now burned in his mind.

As he staggered forward, his mind reeled from what he had seen. The city, the gold, the machine, the monstrous being that wielded power beyond human comprehension. The Spanish steel had been useless, their lead rounds nothing in the face of that ancient force.

He had no doubt now – this city was never meant to be found.

But as he collapsed at the edge of a river, gasping for air, a different thought crept into his mind.

It *must* be found – but only when man is ready.

Only when he has the power to defeat what lurks within.

With bloodied fingers, he opened his book and began to write, sealing away the knowledge in ink and prayer. If no one could wield the power now, then they would have to wait...centuries perhaps. But one day...someone would come.

And when they did, God help them all.

London, England, December 2023

Evelyn Kane pulled her coat tighter against the biting cold and wind as she walked briskly down the crowded London street.

The Christmas lights overhead cast a warm and festive glow, but she barely noticed. She wasn't here to admire the festive decorations. Her mind was on other more pressing things.

She fumbled in her handbag for her compact and flipped it open, pretending to powder her nose as she walked, whilst in reality she was using the small mirror to check to her rear.

There. A man in a dark coat, moving at the same pace as her, just far enough back to not seem obvious. But he was there. He had been for the last three blocks. He didn't try to hide his presence, but he didn't get too close either.

She had no idea who he was, but had her suspicions.

The Crescent Templars, a joint Islamic-Catholic death squad had been after her ever since she had threatened to release 'The Book of Truth' to the press. She had sent copies to religious leaders worldwide, demanding acknowledgment, but her emails had been met with silence. Now, they had resorted to intimidation...but what next?

She exhaled sharply, turning into a small café where Jake and Tariq were already waiting. A bell jingled as she stepped inside, the warmth immediately wrapping around her.

Jake glanced up from his coffee, a look of concern on his face.

"You look like you've seen a ghost," Jake said, raising an eyebrow as he pulled out a chair for her.

"I think I'm being followed," Evelyn muttered, sliding into her seat after planting a soft kiss on Jake's cheek.

Tariq's expression darkened.

"Are you sure?"

She nodded.

"He's been tailing me since I left my office. I took three different routes to make sure I wasn't imagining it, but it's definitely the same man; military posture. He's not just curious - he's hunting".

She looked at them both.

"They're still after 'The Book of Truth'".

Jake leaned back in his chair, folding his arms.

"Whoever *they* are? But you emailed every major religious leader a copy of it. If they weren't going to acknowledge it, I'd have thought they'd just ignore you. But this..." he shook his head, "this means they're scared".

"They are *desperate*," Tariq corrected, "and desperate people do dangerous things".

Evelyn ran a hand through her blonde hair.

"Well, they ransacked my office looking for the book. But they didn't find it".

Jake frowned.

"Where is it?"

A smirk tugged at her lips.

"Wrapped in a different cover – 'Archaeology for Dummies'".

Jake blinked, a half-smile breaking his usual stern expression.

"You're kidding...that's actually bloody brilliant".

Tariq chuckled.

"But what about *our* copies? Do they know about *them*?"

The question made them all pause. The three of them had both their physical copy as well as digital backups of 'The Book of Truth' on encrypted memory sticks, but if the death squad had figured out where Evelyn's office was, how long until they tracked down *their* copies too?

Jake wasn't smiling any more.

"We might need to move those then...and if they know about the book, then they know about us. It won't be long before they try something more direct".

Evelyn nodded.

"Agreed. But first, there's something else".

She pulled out an envelope and placed it on the table.

"This came yesterday. An invitation".

Tariq picked it up and read aloud, *"Miss Evelyn Kane, I would be honoured if you would join me at my estate in Scotland. I have something that may be of interest to you"*.

He frowned as he looked at the signature.

"Who is Lord Dunmore?"

Evelyn's lips pressed into a thin line.

"A Scottish lord with an old family name and a crumbling castle. He says he has a manuscript - a centuries old document detailing the location of a lost city linked to Pizarro".

Jake's eyebrows shot up.

"Pizarro? As in *the* Pizarro, the bloke who conquered the Incas?"

"The very same," Evelyn confirmed, "I'm surprised you know about him".

"Well, I'm not just a pretty face you know," laughed Jake.

Evelyn smiled, then continued.

"Apparently, it wasn't just gold they found in the New World. It was something much older...something not of this Earth".

"Bloody hell...here we go again," said Jake.

Tariq tapped the letter.

"Do you trust him?"

Evelyn hesitated.

"I don't know yet. But we're going to Scotland in the New Year to find out".

Snow dusted the rooftops of the little English village of Wye where Evelyn Kane called home. Twinkling fairy lights glowed in the cold evening air, and the scent of mulled wine and roasting chestnuts drifted through the cobbled streets. It was Christmas Eve, and despite everything - the dangers, the secrets, the looming possibility of an expedition - tonight was about family, friends, and a rare moment of peace.

Evelyn stood at the window of her cosy, but large, cottage, watching as Jake's car pulled into the driveway. He stepped out, stretching his legs after the long drive, and slung his duffel bag over one broad shoulder. Dressed in jeans and a leather jacket, he looked every bit the soldier turned private contractor, but when he saw her, a slow smile spread across his face.

She opened the door before he could knock.

"Took you long enough".

Jake smirked.

"Traffic. *And* I had to stop and pick this up".

He handed her a bottle of whisky, a rich, peaty single malt from Scotland.

"I thought we might need it, you know, being Christmas and all that".

Evelyn laughed, stepping aside to let him in.

"You know me too well".

He set his bag down and pulled her into a firm, warm hug.

"Well, we've been together for over a year now mate...Merry Christmas, Evie".

She tilted her head up, pressing a soft kiss to his lips.

"Merry Christmas, Jake".

The smell of fresh tea and cinnamon filled the air as Evelyn set the table for breakfast. Outside, the village was blanketed in snow, the world hushed in the quiet of Christmas morning.

Jake appeared in the doorway, barefoot, wearing a t-shirt and the flannel pyjama bottoms she had bought him last Christmas as a joke.

"I still think these are ridiculous," he said, looking down at the red and green plaid pattern.

Evelyn smirked.

"And yet, you wear them".

"Only because I love you," he muttered, pouring the freshly made tea into their two cups.

She chuckled.

"Mmm-hmm...love eh? Come on then...open your presents".

They exchanged gifts by the fireplace, the tree twinkling beside them. Jake unwrapped a sleek new knife, a custom made combat blade Evelyn had sourced from a local blacksmith.

He ran his thumb over the engraved initials.

"Perfect".

Evelyn opened a small box and gasped. Inside was an antique gold locket. She clicked it open to find an old map fragment folded inside.

Jake leaned in, smirking.

"Thought it might come in handy".

"You got me *treasure* for Christmas?"

"Wouldn't be us if I didn't".

She kissed him, slow and deep.

"Best Christmas ever".

By midday, the house was filled with the rich aroma of roasted turkey, buttery potatoes, and spiced vegetables. Tariq arrived with his wife, Miriam, and their two children, Omar and Asmaan, who ran inside excitedly, bundled up in coats and scarves.

"Merry Christmas!" Miriam greeted, hugging Evelyn warmly.

"Merry Christmas! Come in, get warm".

Tariq grinned as he set down a bottle of champagne.

"We thought we would embrace the season...a little in moderation. The children are excited for presents".

Jake ruffled Omar's hair.

"Have you been good this year, mate?"

Omar grinned.

"Father Christmas says yes."

Tariq chuckled.

"*He* says yes, but let us just say Santa and I may have different opinions".

Everyone laughed as they settled around the table. The meal was loud and warm, full of conversation, laughter, and clinking glasses. Miriam and Evelyn debated the best way to cook stuffing, while Jake and Tariq traded playful jabs about the last time they had been in Afghanistan together.

After dinner, they gathered around the fire for presents. The children tore into their gifts - model aeroplanes for Omar, a beautiful handmade doll for Asmaan. Tariq surprised Evelyn with a stunning silk scarf, while Jake presented Tariq with a finely crafted fountain pen.

"I suppose this is meant to encourage my academic side," Tariq mused.

Jake grinned.

"You need to look the part, *Professor*".

As the fire crackled in the hearth, casting flickering shadows on the walls, the group lounged comfortably in the living room, bellies full from the feast. Outside, the village was quiet, the snow-covered rooftops reflecting the glow of festive lights. Omar and Asmaan sat cross-legged by the Christmas tree, playing with their new toys, while Miriam cradled a steaming cup of tea, smiling at the sight of her children's excitement.

Evelyn curled up next to Jake on the sofa, her head resting lightly on his shoulder, whilst Tariq sank back in his chair, stretching his legs out, a rare moment of relaxation visible on his face.

She glanced at him.

"So, Tariq...what does Christmas mean to you and your family? I know it's not a religious thing for you, but you seem to embrace it".

Tariq gave a thoughtful sigh as he watched the flames dance in the fireplace.

"You are right. As Muslims, we do not celebrate Christmas as a religious holiday. But that does not mean we do not appreciate it...when in Rome, as they say".

He gestured toward Miriam.

"When we were growing up, we had Christian friends who always included us in their celebrations. The warmth, the generosity, the joy – it is infectious. And, at its heart, it is about family and togetherness, which is something we *do* value deeply in Islam".

Miriam nodded, smiling.

"It is also a time of giving, of showing kindness to others. That is something that transcends religion. In our culture, charity and hospitality are fundamental. We love seeing the children happy, sharing good food with friends, and taking a break from the chaos of the world".

Jake chuckled.

"So basically, you like the presents and the feast?"

Tariq smirked.

"Obviously. And the terrible Christmas music playing in every shop from October onward".

"Terrible? Come on I love Christmas music, it's all part of the fun," replied Jake.

Miriam groaned.

"Do not remind me. Omar has been singing *Jingle Bells* since November".

Evelyn laughed.

"That's completely normal. Jake, remember the army barracks at Christmas? Someone always had a radio blasting *Last Christmas* on repeat".

Jake rolled his eyes.

"And by New Year's Day, we all wanted to burn the damn thing".

Omar, who had been half-listening, piped up.

"Baba says Father Christmas doesn't visit Muslim houses".

Tariq sighed and gave his son a look.

"*I* said that Father Christmas traditionally visits Christian children, but I never said he would not visit you if you were good".

Asmaan, hugging her doll, beamed.

"So he *does* visit?"

Miriam laughed and ruffled her daughter's hair.

"Well, there *were* presents under the tree this morning, were there not?"

Omar narrowed his eyes.

"That could have been *you*".

Jake bent forward, lowering his voice conspiratorially.

"Or...maybe your dad is one of Santa's secret helpers".

Omar's eyes widened.

"Really?"

Tariq sighed dramatically.

"Thank you Jake...I think".

Evelyn grinned.

"I bet the *real* Santa has people like you on his team. You know, to handle the 'naughty list' situations".

Jake smirked.

"Elf squad tactics".

The room burst into laughter.

Miriam sipped her tea, smiling.

"You see? This is what I love about Christmas. It brings people together, regardless of faith or background. It is about kindness, laughter, and a little bit of magic".

Tariq nodded.

"And, of course, an excellent excuse to eat too much and fall asleep on the sofa".

"Which is exactly what you're about to do," Evelyn teased.

Tariq yawned, stretching his arms.

"I cannot deny it".

As the evening wound down, Evelyn watched the flickering flames and the contentment on her friends' faces; laughter, and warmth, the kind of rare peace that Evelyn knew wouldn't last. In January, a new adventure would begin. But tonight, it was Christmas, and, in this little house filled with love and friendship, that was all that mattered.

CHAPTER 2

FAMILY TIES

The journey from the airport took them north through the snow-covered Highlands, a breathtaking expanse of rolling hills and rounded peaks dusted in white. The landscape was both beautiful and unforgiving, the skeletal branches of pine trees bending under the weight of freshly fallen snow. Frozen lochs reflected the pale winter sun, their glassy surfaces broken only by the occasional ripple of movement beneath the ice.

Jake drove the hired Range Rover along the winding roads, the occasional flurry of snow dancing in the headlights. Evelyn sat beside him, gazing out at the scenery, her breath fogging the glass as she pressed her fingers against the warmth of the heater. In the back seat, Tariq checked his phone, but there was barely any signal - just as he expected in the depths of the Scottish Highlands.

"This place is incredible," Evelyn murmured, watching as a herd of deer emerged from the trees, their antlers stark against the white backdrop, "it's like stepping into a postcard."

"A freezing cold postcard," Tariq muttered, pulling his coat tighter around him, "why did I agree to this again?"

"Adventure," Jake grinned, "besides, you didn't have much choice. Evelyn would have dragged you here. Anyway, it's a bit different to Afghanistan; at least no one is trying to kill us here".

As Jake finished his sentence a rabbit suddenly appeared in the centre of the road and Jake quickly slammed on the brakes causing the vehicle to come to a skidding halt.

Evelyn smirked.

"What was that you were saying?"

The road wound higher into the hills, the terrain becoming more rugged. Ancient stone bridges arched over rushing rivers, their surfaces caked with ice. Small villages with smoke curling from chimneys sat nestled in valleys, the soft glow of their lights visible through the thickening dusk. The occasional pub, its windows glowing amber, promised warmth and whisky to weary travellers, but they had no time to stop.

As the sun dipped below the horizon, they rounded a bend - and there it was.

Lord Dunmore's castle.

Perched atop a craggy hill, the fortress loomed over the surrounding land, its stone walls blackened by age and weather. Towers and turrets reached skyward like giant's fingers, their pointed roofs capped with snow. The vast structure was a blend of medieval strength and Victorian opulence, its sheer size making it clear that Dunmore's ancestors had once wielded considerable power.

Lights burned in several windows, flickering like beacons against the twilight. The long, winding driveway was flanked by towering yew trees, their branches heavy with snow. Stone gargoyles, frozen in time, watched from their perches along the battlements, their grotesque faces partially obscured by icicles.

"Bloody hell," Jake muttered, slowing the car, "now that's a *proper* castle".

Tariq exhaled.

"I hope it does not have any ghosts".

Evelyn grinned.

"You never know. Lord Dunmore might have one locked up in the cellar".

The Range Rover crunched over the slushy gravel drive, its headlights illuminating the massive oak doors at the castle's entrance. Two lantern lights flanked the doorway, their glow casting long shadows against the stone. A butler, dressed in a heavy overcoat, stepped forward as they pulled to a stop.

"Welcome to Dunmore Castle," he intoned, his voice echoing in the cold night air, "the Laird is expecting you".

Jake turned off the engine, and for a moment, the only sound was the distant cry of an owl somewhere in the trees.

Evelyn shivered slightly, though not entirely from the cold.

Something about this place felt *heavy*, as though the very stones held secrets that had long been buried beneath the frost.

The great oak doors creaked open, revealing a vast entrance hall lit by the warm glow of chandeliers suspended from the high vaulted ceiling. The scent of burning coal and aged leather filled the air, mingling with the faint tang of cold stone. Thick intricate tapestries lined the walls, depicting ancient battles and long-forgotten hunts, their colours faded but still striking. A grand staircase, its mahogany bannister polished to a gleaming shine, spiralled upward to the upper floors.

The butler stepped aside, gesturing for them to enter. He was an elderly man, perhaps in his sixties, with silvered hair neatly combed back, and sharp, observant eyes. His livery - a black suit with a stiff white collar - was immaculate, though Evelyn noted his hands bore the calluses of a man used to hard work.

"I am Henshaw, Lord Dunmore's butler," he said in a clear English accent, "his Lordship awaits you in the drawing room. If you will allow me, I shall have your luggage taken to your rooms".

Two footmen in dark livery appeared as if on cue, taking their bags with silent efficiency before disappearing down a long corridor.

"Thank you," Evelyn replied, unbuttoning her coat.

Henshaw held out his arm for their coats and to indicate their direction of travel.

"This way, please".

They followed him through the grand hall, their footsteps echoing against the stone floor. Mounted suits of armour lined the passage, their visors staring blankly ahead as if watching unseen guests pass through the centuries. The flickering bulbs in the lamps played tricks on the polished metal, making it seem as if the knights might move at any moment.

Jake leaned toward Evelyn.

"This place has *atmosphere*".

Evelyn smirked.

"That's one way to put it".

At the end of the corridor, Henshaw pushed open a heavy wooden door and stepped aside.

The drawing room was a stark contrast to the imposing entrance hall. Richly furnished with deep leather armchairs, a roaring fire crackling in the stone hearth, and shelves upon shelves of old books, it exuded warmth and quiet luxury. A grand piano sat in the corner, and oil paintings of Dunmore ancestors lined the walls, their stern faces gazing down at the newcomers. A decanter of whisky and crystal glasses sat on a side table, next to a tray of delicate canapés.

And, in the centre of the room, stood Lord Dunmore.

Tall and lean, with sharp aristocratic features and red curly hair, he carried himself with effortless authority. His dark green tweed jacket and polished leather boots spoke of old wealth, but there was a keen intelligence in his eyes that suggested he was more than just a relic of the past.

"Ah, Miss Kane," he said, stepping forward with an easy smile, "we meet at last".

He extended a hand, and Evelyn shook it firmly.

"It's a pleasure, Lord Dunmore".

"Please, just Alexander, or Alex. Titles are for Parliament and dusty history books".

He turned to Jake and Tariq, giving them an appraising look.

"And you must be Captain Allsop and Doctor Ahmed".

Jake gave a half-smile.

"Er...Sergeant Major actually sir, but it's just Jake now".

Tariq nodded.

"And Tariq will do fine".

Dunmore grinned.

"Excellent. I was hoping for informality. Now, please, sit. Have a drink. You must be frozen after your journey".

As they settled into the plush chairs, Evelyn studied the man carefully. There was something charming about him, but also something measured - like a chess player always thinking several moves ahead.

And in a place like this, she thought, that probably wasn't a coincidence.

She sipped her whisky, letting the warmth settle in her chest before setting the glass down on the polished mahogany table. She leaned forward slightly, fixing Dunmore with a steely eyed gaze.

"You've been rather mysterious about why we're here, Lord Dunmore..."

"Alex, please."

He smiled, though there was an edge of calculation behind it.

"Alright...Alex," Evelyn replied, "why don't you tell us exactly why you invited us here?"

Dunmore reached to the side table and lifted a heavy, leather-bound book. It was old, centuries old, its cracked brown cover held together with a brass clasp. The edges of the pages were brittle and yellowed, and a strange emblem was branded into the leather: a stylized sun with jagged rays. He placed it carefully on the table between them.

"This," he said, tapping the book with one long finger, "is the reason you're here".

Tariq raised his eyebrows.

"What is it?"

Dunmore unclasped the book and carefully turned a few of the fragile pages.

"A journal," he said, "written by a Spanish monk in the early sixteenth century. He was the sole survivor of a massacre deep in the South American jungle - one carried out by something more than just native warriors".

Evelyn's interest sharpened.

"Where did *you* get it?"

Dunmore smiled.

"It has been in my family for generations. You see, my ancestor - Alexander, the third Earl of Dunmore - took a Spanish bride. She brought a great many things with her, including this journal, which was said to have been smuggled out of Spain by a disgraced nobleman. It has passed from heir to heir ever since, but until now, no one has really bothered to read it or act on what it contains".

Jake's curiosity was evident.

"And what exactly *does* it contain?"

Dunmore sighed, running a hand over the brittle parchment.

"The last testament of a dying man. A man who claimed to have seen an untouched city of gold hidden deep in the jungle.

He wrote of a machine housed within its temple, something beyond the understanding of the Spanish at the time, which appeared to have no power source. He described vessels on the walls that radiated light - not flames or candles, but something else entirely. He also wrote of how the Conquistadors were slaughtered, every last one of them, except for him. Whatever killed them...he didn't describe it in detail, only that it was 'not of this world'".

A heavy silence settled over the room.

Evelyn drummed her fingers against the armrest of her chair.

"So, you believe this machine is still there?"

Dunmore's lips curled into a confident smile.

"I *know* it is. And I want it, for I believe it could be a kinetically powered generator of some sort, and you know how sought after that is in these times".

"Of course you do," Jake thought to himself.

He then raised an eyebrow.

"And the gold?"

Dunmore waved a hand.

"You can take it. Gold is valuable, but something that produces energy without fuel? That is wealth beyond measure".

Evelyn crossed her legs and rested her hands in her lap.

"If we're going to do this, we're going to need resources - supplies, transport, and equipment. Everything. And our price is fifty percent of the find, plus our expenses".

She let the words settle before adding, "*Including* the machine".

Dunmore's expression tightened, the flicker of annoyance breaking through his aristocratic charm.

"That is rather steep, Miss Kane".

"It's non-negotiable," she said coolly, "an expedition like this isn't just a matter of jumping on a plane and wandering through the jungle. It takes logistics, planning, and - most importantly - risk. And if we're risking our lives, we get an equal share".

"Well, it's not really an equal share is it?" Jake added, "Us three get a third of fifty per cent".

Dunmore tapped his fingers against the arm of his chair, considering. The fire crackled in the hearth, casting shifting shadows along the walls. Finally, he gave out a sigh and slowly nodded.

"Very well," he said, "it seems we are to be partners".

Jake smirked.

"Glad we could come to an understanding".

Dunmore stood, swirling his whisky in the glass before finishing it in one smooth motion, and pouring himself another glass.

"I take it you will make the necessary arrangements? Departure in say...two weeks?" Oh, and one more thing..." he set the empty glass down and gave them a measured look, "I'm coming with you".

"That might complicate things," replied Evelyn.

Dunmore smiled.

"I think it makes them *far* more interesting".

Evelyn folded her arms and leaned back in her chair, studying Dunmore with a sceptical eye. The fire crackled behind her, its warmth doing little to soften her tone.

"You do realise that we're not heading off on a luxury hunting trip, don't you?" she asked, "the jungle isn't some gentleman's playground - it's a brutal, hostile environment. Do you have *any* experience operating in that kind of terrain? Or in any kind of hostile situation?"

Dunmore gave her a wry smile and took a slow sip of his whisky before answering.

"I was training to be an officer at Sandhurst," he admitted, "I made it through most of the course before my father died, but I had to resign before commissioning due to inheriting the title and all the responsibilities that came with it".

Jake, leaning casually against the mantelpiece, exchanged a glance with Tariq.

"So that's a no, then," he said, smirking.

Dunmore exhaled, setting his glass down.

"Let's just say I'm not completely useless. I know how to handle a rifle, and I'm not afraid of getting my hands dirty".

"Handling a rifle at a shooting range and carrying one through a jungle filled with things that want to kill you are two different experiences," Jake pointed out, "snakes, big cats, disease, hostile locals...not to mention the fact that if there's treasure involved, we probably won't be the only ones looking for it".

Evelyn sighed, rubbing her temple.

"Look, we're not saying you *can't* come. But you need to understand what you're getting in to. This is going to be dangerous. There's no backup, no cavalry. If things go sideways, we have to rely on each other".

Dunmore nodded.

"Understood. I still want in. I *am* funding this thing, after all".

Jake let out a low whistle.

"Well, at least he's got balls," he muttered to Evelyn, "I suppose we'll just have to keep an eye on him".

Evelyn turned back to Dunmore.

"Fine. But don't expect us to hold your hand out there".

A few days later, the team gathered in Evelyn's office in London. The walls were covered in maps, satellite images, and old manuscripts, while Jake and Tariq had stacked various books on the desk, searching for any historical records that might help them locate the lost city.

"We're looking at a region of the Andes that's barely been touched," Evelyn said, tracing a finger along a faded map, "most of the old Spanish accounts are vague - either because they didn't know exactly where they were, or they deliberately left out details to keep others from finding the gold".

"And then they all died before they could return," Jake added, "that's always a great sign".

Tariq tapped on a more modern topographical map.

"But this area? It is full of ruins. Some already explored, some barely touched. If this manuscript is accurate, we need to head somewhere between these three locations..."

He pointed at three spots deep in the jungle.

"...which means we will need the right equipment to even get there".

"That brings us very nicely to weapons and supplies," Jake said, "we can't just wander in with backpacks and a compass. We need firepower, survival gear, and transport".

He reached for his phone and flicked through his list of contacts.

"I've got a mate in Belize...ex-military, runs a little 'business' on the side. He can sort us out with weapons and other useful kit before we head into Peru".

Evelyn nodded.

"Good. We'll also need guides, maybe some local muscle. Money won't be an issue, thanks to Lord Dunmore's deep pockets".

Dunmore, lounging in a chair with a drink in hand, smirked.

"See? I *am* useful".

Jake rolled his eyes.

"Well, that has yet to be seen".

Tariq turned to Evelyn and spoke in a low voice.

"We should probably keep our movements quiet. If we are being watched, we do not want certain people knowing our plans".

Evelyn glanced at the disguised book on her shelf. Their last encounter with the Crescent Templars was quite tame, but there was no doubt that if their enemies found out what they were searching for now, the hunt would become even deadlier.

The engines of the sleek private jet hummed smoothly as it soared above the clouds, leaving behind the grey winter skies of England. From the small airfield in Kent, the aircraft had taken off without fanfare, cutting a quiet path across the Atlantic. The luxury of the cabin, with its polished wood panelling, plush leather seats, and soft lighting, was a stark contrast to the brutal conditions the group would soon be facing in the jungle.

Evelyn sat by the window, gazing at the endless blue below. She had a glass of water in one hand and a tablet in the other, scrolling through maps and notes. The manuscript lay open on the table in front of her, old parchment pages covered in delicate, precise script.

Jake stretched out in his seat across from her, boots propped up on the edge of the table despite the disapproving look from Dunmore.

"So, let's talk about what happens when we land. Your fellow in Belize, Jake...how reliable is he?"

Jake smirked.

"As reliable as someone in the arms trade can be. He's ex-British Army, did some work for private contractors, then set up shop in Central America. He can get us weapons, satcoms, whatever we need".

Tariq, seated next to him, raised an eyebrow.

"And we can trust him?"

"We don't *trust* anyone," Jake said, "but money talks, and I've worked with him before. He'll get us what we need...no questions asked".

Lord Dunmore, reclining in his seat with a glass of whisky, glanced over.

"I hope we're not wasting time in Belize. The sooner we get to Peru, the better".

"Not a waste," Evelyn said without looking up, "we need the right equipment, and Belize is our best stop for that. Plus, Jake's contact can set us up with transport in Peru".

Dunmore sighed.

"Fine. But let's not linger longer than necessary".

Outside, the sun was setting, casting a golden glow over the vast ocean below. They were flying thousands of feet above the world, but Evelyn couldn't shake the feeling that danger was already closing in on them.

As the flight continued, the group fell into quiet preparation. Evelyn reviewed the journal, Tariq studied topographical maps, Jake cleaned his pistol - more out of habit than necessity - and Dunmore, after finishing his drink, stared out the window, lost in thought.

A few hours later, the jet began its descent. Below them, the runway lights of Philip S.W. Goldson International Airport twinkled against the darkening landscape of Belize. As the wheels touched down on the tarmac, Evelyn took a deep breath.

The easy part was over. Now, the real adventure was about to begin.

CHAPTER 3

A STICKY
SITUATION

The jet's wheels kissed the tarmac with a smooth precision, the engines whistling as the aircraft slowed and turned off the main runway. Instead of heading toward the busy terminal, the pilot followed instructions to taxi toward a secluded hangar on the far side of the airfield, away from customs, security, and prying eyes. The hangar doors were already open, revealing a handful of figures waiting in the dim light.

As the aircraft came to a halt, the cabin door hissed open, and the steps deployed. Warm, humid air rushed inside, carrying the scent of the tropics - damp earth, diesel fumes, and the distant tang of salt from the Caribbean. Although it was dark outside the heat was stifling, a sticky sort of heat which hit the group as soon as the aircraft's door opened.

At the bottom of the steps stood Ed Pinkard, or *Pinky* as he was known to his mates. He was a broad shouldered man in his late forties, his tanned face lined from years in the sun, a thick ginger-streaked beard framing his sharp features. Despite the humidity, he wore a lightweight field jacket over a faded t-shirt, and his stance - relaxed but alert - marked him as a man who had never truly left the battlefield.

Jake was the first down the steps.

"Jesus, Pinky, you've let yourself go".

Pinky grinned and grabbed Jake into a bear hug.

"You cheeky bastard. I'm still handsome enough to knock you on your arse mate".

They separated, slapping each other on the back before Pinky turned to the others.

"Welcome to Belize. So who have we got here then?"

Jake gestured behind him.

This is Evelyn Kane, the brains of the outfit, and Tariq Ahmed, *you* remember him from Afghanistan? And that over there is Lord Alexander Dunmore".

Pinky raised an eyebrow at the last introduction but said nothing. Instead, he stuck out his hand to Evelyn and Tariq.

"Good to meet you Evelyn, and Tariq good to see you again...and Your Lordship," he added with a half bow and a grin as Dunmore descended the steps, looking around with mild distaste at the humid airfield.

"Let's get moving," Pinky said, "I've got a couple of vehicles waiting. Don't want to be hanging around here longer than necessary".

The group grabbed their bags as Pinky led them to two black Land Rovers parked just inside the hangar. They stowed their luggage in one of the vehicles, and the moment they were inside, they pulled away, slipping out through a side gate and onto a darkened service road.

Pinky was at the wheel, Jake riding in the front passenger seat, while the others sat in the back. As they passed a row of old, faded barracks, Pinky let out a chuckle.

"Bloody hell, do you remember that place?" he said, nodding toward the compound.

Jake grinned.

"Yeah. Price Barracks. Spent too many nights sweating my arse off in those buildings that's for sure".

"Patrolling the border, keeping the Guatemalans from trying their luck," Pinky mused, "and then there were the jungle ops - tracking cartel bastards through the bush. Jesus, it was a bloody mess".

Jake nodded, his mind drifting back over a decade.

"We did some good, though. Busted a few of their safe houses, destroyed their plantations, put a couple of their big boys in the ground".

Pinky grunted.

"And how many more just took their place? You know how it works. These bastards don't disappear. They just change faces".

Jake leaned back.

"Still... it wasn't a bad life. Good work, good lads".

Pinky shot him a side glance.

"Do you miss it?"

Jake smirked.

"Sometimes. Then I remember the heat, the insects, and the smell of a rotting jungle corpse, and I think...maybe not".

Pinky laughed.

"Aye, you never forget *that* smell."

Evelyn, listening from the back, watched the two men with interest. There was a bond between them that only came from years of shared danger. She had known Jake had spent time in Belize during his Army years, but hearing the two men reminisce made it all seem more real - less like a story, more like something still lurking in their memories.

As they drove toward the city, the streetlights flickered through the windows, illuminating the buildings mixed with modern storefronts and palm-lined streets. It was a lively place, bustling even at night, the streets of Belize City alive with movement, the air, thick with humidity, carrying the scent of the sea, mingling with the smoky aroma of street vendors grilling meat on open fires.

The roads were uneven, cracked in places from years of tropical downpours. Neon lights flickered over shopfronts selling everything from fresh fruit to second hand electronics. Market stalls lined the pavements, where vendors shouted out the day's final deals in a mix of English, Spanish and Kriol. A battered old school bus, repurposed as public transport, roared past, packed with locals heading home.

Motorcycles weaved between cars, their riders wearing loose shirts that flapped in the warm breeze. A few children kicked a football along a side street, laughing as it bounced unpredictably over the potholes, whilst music blasted from open doorways - reggae, punta and Spanish pop blending into a chaotic yet vibrant melody.

As they approached Swing Bridge, the oldest manually operated bridge in Central America, the water below shimmered with reflections from streetlights. Small fishing boats bobbed in the slow current, their decks piled with nets and plastic containers. A pelican sat motionless on a wooden piling, waiting for a chance to snatch a meal from the returning boats.

Further into town, Pinky navigated past old colonial-era buildings - faded but still standing strong with their whitewashed walls and wooden balconies. Some had been converted into hotels or bars, their doors open to welcome tourists escaping the cold northern winter. Caye Caulker and Ambergris Caye - the famous islands off the coast - were on every travel poster they passed, advertising white sandy beaches and turquoise waters.

Jake watched the streets with a knowing gaze, the memories of past missions surfacing. He remembered nights spent in bars near Marine Parade, the tension of border patrols in the jungle, and the adrenaline rush of tracking cartel smugglers through the dense undergrowth.

Evelyn, taking it all in for the first time, was intrigued.

"It's...it's a crazy place," she murmured, watching a group of men lounging outside a rum shop, smoking cigars and laughing.

Pinky chuckled.

"That's Belize for you. A bit rough around the edges, but it's got its charm".

The small convoy turned onto Princess Margaret Drive, leaving behind the bustling streets and heading toward the quieter, more affluent side of the city. Their destination soon came into view – a high end hotel near the waterfront, its white façade glowing under golden lights.

As they pulled into the private driveway, a uniformed doorman stepped forward to greet them. The city's energy faded behind them, replaced by the cool, air-conditioned luxury of the hotel.

"Enjoy the comfort while you can," Pinky said as he helped unload the second vehicle, "we've got a lot to do tomorrow".

The Grand Belize Hotel stood proudly along the city's waterfront, like a beacon of colonial elegance against the humid, tropical night, a building that had been carefully restored to its former glory. Its white stucco walls, trimmed with dark mahogany beams, gleamed under the soft glow of vintage lanterns, giving it an air of old-world charm, while large shuttered windows, framed by creeping bougainvillea added splashes of deep red and purple, as they reflected the twinkling lights of the harbour. The wide verandah was lined with whirring ceiling fans, and overlooked the bustling streets of Belize City, where the sounds of distant music, occasional honking horns, and the murmur of conversation drifted through the night air. Tall palm trees lined the driveway, their fronds rustling in the evening breeze, while the neatly manicured gardens were dotted with exotic flowers whose fragrance carried on the humid night air.

A wide stone staircase led up to the entrance, flanked by bronze statues of jaguars, their eyes catching the light as if they were watching every guest who arrived. At the top of the steps, the grand mahogany double doors stood open, revealing a warmly lit lobby beyond. A uniformed doorman, his white gloves pristine against the dark fabric of his jacket, tipped his hat as he pulled open the door for them.

Beyond the hotel, the Caribbean Sea stretched into the horizon, its calm surface reflecting the moonlight in shimmering ripples. The scent of salt and distant cooking fires mingled with the faintest hint of cigar smoke drifting from the terrace bar, where guests lounged with cocktails in hand, enjoying the balmy evening.

Inside, the cool air conditioned lobby was a world away from the sticky heat outside. The walls were adorned with oil paintings of 18th century Spanish galleons, and polished marble floors reflected the glow of crystal chandeliers. A massive mahogany reception desk stood at the centre, behind which a smiling receptionist in a smart uniform greeted them.

"Welcome to the Grand Belize Hotel. How may I assist you?"

Jake stepped forward.

"We have reservations under Evelyn Kane".

The receptionist checked her ledger, then slid three brass room keys across the counter.

"Here you go. The bellboy will take your luggage. Enjoy your stay".

"I think I shall retire upstairs. It's been a long day," Dunmore announced as he bid everyone goodnight.

A young bellboy in a neatly pressed white jacket appeared, and was already loading their bags onto a trolley. But Jake had stopped listening.

Across the dimly lit lounge, a man sat alone in a high backed leather armchair, facing away from them. He had one booted foot resting on the low table, a glass of rum and coke in his hand. His broad shoulders, the short blonde hair, and the unmistakable air of someone who had been through hell and walked out grinning were instantly recognisable.

Jake nudged Evelyn and Tariq.

"There he is".

The man turned slightly, and the light caught his face – Lecky.

Former US Army Special Forces; a survivor of every war zone of the 21st century, that chewed men up and spat them out. The last time they had seen him was at Kabul Airport, during the chaos of the Taliban takeover. They had barely escaped with their lives after discovering The Garden of Eden - a place that still haunted all of them; but in a good way.

As they approached, Lecky looked up, his steel blue eyes locking onto them. A slow grin spread across his face.

"Well, I'll be damned," he said, standing up and clasping Jake's hand in a firm shake, "I got your call, and here I am...not sure why though".

Jake smiled.

"I didn't think you'd pass up an adventure".

Lecky chuckled.

"Not when *you're* involved, and definitely not when someone sends me *this*" he replied as he reached in to his jacket pocket and produced an unsigned cheque to the value of $50,000. "I don't suppose you can sign it now can you Jake?"

"That's Evelyn's department mate, she's the money bags here," replied Jake.

Tariq grinned, shaking Lecky's hand.

"Good to see you my friend".

"Salaam Tariq jaan. Chotor asti, khub asti?" Lecky enquired.

"Thank you for asking. I am very well, and your Dari is very good," replied Tariq.

Lecky smiled in appreciation, then he turned to Evelyn, his grin shifting into something softer as he took hold her hand and kissed it.

"Miss Kane...looking as beautiful as ever".

Evelyn blushed as she turned her gaze to Jake and Tariq.

"At last, someone to keep these two out of trouble".

"Steady!" laughed Jake.

"More like lead them into it," he joked as he gestured to the empty chairs around his table, "come on, take a seat and tell me what type of hell you've gotten me into this time".

The three of them took their seats as Lecky leaned back in his chair, swirling the ice in his drink. His eyes flicked between them, waiting for the big reveal.

Evelyn didn't waste time.

"We're going after a lost city in the Peruvian jungle".

Lecky raised an eyebrow but said nothing.

"Not just any lost city," Jake added, "a Spanish expedition found it centuries ago, filled with more gold than they could carry apparently".

Lecky pondered for a moment.

"So why didn't the *Spaniards* carry it out then?"

Tariq, Evelyn and Jake cast brief glances at each other.

Lecky exhaled, shaking his head with a grin.

"You had me at 'gold,' but your strange looks have made me think of all the ways this could go south. I take it they didn't make it out then?"

He took a sip of his drink.

"Still, I'm listening".

"We have a map and a journal from that Spanish expedition. It details how they found the city and - more importantly - what stopped them from leaving," Evelyn explained.

Lecky's grin faltered slightly.

"Go on".

Jake smirked.

"You ever hear of a treasure so big, even the people who found it didn't live to tell the tale?"

Lecky let out a low whistle.

"Plenty of myths, legends, but if you've got hard proof..."

"We do," Evelyn assured him, "and we know what we're looking for. The gold is one thing, but there's something else".

Evelyn exchanged a glance with Jake before continuing.

"There's a machine. We're not sure what it is yet, but the journal describes it as something beyond anything the Spanish had ever seen".

"A machine? In a lost city? That *is* wild," exclaimed Lecky.

Evelyn nodded.

"Something ancient, powerful...maybe even alien in origin".

Lecky exhaled sharply and sat back.

"You weren't kidding about hell".

Then his smirk returned.

"But you also weren't kidding about wealth, were you?"

Jake grinned.

"We get half of whatever we find".

Lecky let out a short laugh as he did some calculations in his head.

"So we get twelve and a half percent each? I like those odds".

He took another sip of his drink, then eyed them suspiciously.

"But that brings me to my next question... who gets the other fifty percent...and why the hell are we in Belize?"

Jake chuckled to himself.

"That's two questions mate. Lord Dunmore is the expedition sponsor...benefactor...and he gets the big cut...you'll meet him tomorrow; and, as for being here, we need more than just a couple of maps and a dream to pull this off. We need weapons, supplies, and transport".

Lecky nodded slowly.

"And you know a guy?"

Jake grinned.

"I know a guy".

Lecky laughed, shaking his head.

"Of course you do".

He lifted his glass.

"Well then, here's to another death-defying adventure".

Evelyn clinked her glass against his.

"Let's just hope this one ends with us richer than last time".

Lecky almost choked on his drink.

"Whoa now...what are you talking about? All I got was my *army* pay...what did I miss?"

Evelyn and Tariq exchanged a look. She sighed, and then turned back to Lecky.

"Tariq and I found an ancient mine deep in Nuristan. Sapphires, rubies, emeralds...all sorts".

Lecky shook his head in disbelief.

"And you two just...walked out of there rich?"

Jake chuckled.

"They were already loaded before they even met us, mate".

Lecky let out another low whistle, shaking his head in amazement.

"So, let me get this straight...you two had millions in gemstones stuffed in your packs the whole time we were slogging through the mountains, dodging bullets and lunatics?"

"Pretty much," Evelyn admitted.

Lecky gave a short laugh, leaning back in his chair.

"And here I was, thinking we were all just scraping by, trying to stay alive. Meanwhile, you two were carrying enough wealth to buy your own country".

Jake grinned.

"Told you they were smarter than us".

"We were," Evelyn assured him, "the Eden find was something else. No amount of money could compare to that".

Lecky snorted.

"Money doesn't buy paradise, but it sure as hell makes the rest of the world easier to live in".

"I feel guilty now," said Evelyn in a low voice.

Lecky slapped Evelyn on the back.

"Ha! I'm only kidding. But I don't know whether to be impressed or envious".

He sat back, rubbing his chin, glanced at the cheque still sitting on the table, then picked it up and twirled it between his fingers, before letting out a long sigh.

"Fifty grand's a good start".

Then his eyes gleamed.

"But if this Peruvian haul is half as good as you say it is, I expect to walk away with a hell of a lot more".

Jake grinned.

"Stick with us, mate. You'll get your payday".

Lecky knocked back the rest of his drink and set the glass down with a decisive clink.

"Then what are we waiting for?"

The next morning, after a breakfast of tea and fresh fruit on the hotel's terrace, the group gathered in the lobby to introduce Lecky to Lord Dunmore. The Scottish nobleman stood stiffly, his hands clasped behind his back, his expression one of thinly veiled disapproval as he appraised the American.

Lecky, for his part, had seen this look before - the kind that aristocrats reserved for those they considered uncultured. He grinned, extending a hand.

"Lecky".

Dunmore hesitated a fraction too long before shaking it.

"Lord Dunmore," he said curtly, "I suppose you'll be another set of hands for this endeavour".

Lecky held his grin, detecting the hint of condescension.

"Something like that".

The lord's gaze flicked to Jake and Evelyn, as if silently questioning why they needed another soldier. Evelyn, sensing the tension, quickly changed the subject.

"We should get moving. Pinky's expecting us".

They climbed into a pair of dusty SUVs and set off, weaving through the chaotic streets of Belize City. The air was thick with humidity, the scent of the sea battling with exhaust fumes. Market stalls lined the roads, selling everything from woven blankets to fresh fish, while the ever-present local music beats pulsed from open shopfronts.

Soon, the city thinned, giving way to industrial lots and rundown warehouses. Their destination was a large metal hangar at the end of a secluded road. Pinky stood outside, arms folded, wearing a faded khaki shirt and cargo pants. He greeted them with a broad grin.

"Well, well, look what the cat dragged in," he said, giving Jake a firm handshake.

He led them inside, where stacks of crates filled the space. Weapons, survival gear, medical supplies, even a few crates labelled *High Explosives* sat waiting. A Cessna Caravan light aircraft was parked in the far corner, its side hatch open, revealing more gear inside.

Jake whistled.

"You've done us proud here mate".

Pinky shrugged.

"I figured you'd need the best. This lot should see you through the jungle - M4s, side arms, ammo, rations, night vision, the works".

He patted one of the crates.

"And a few surprises."

"And the aircraft?" Evelyn enquired.

Pinky nodded towards the Cessna.

"Pilot's on standby. He'll take you to a jungle airstrip near Puerto Maldonado in Peru. From there, I've arranged for a Land Rover to get you deeper in-country. Safe spot to stash the plane too - no customs, no questions".

Lecky was impressed.

"You've sure been busy".

Pinky grinned.

"I like to keep my friends well armed".

Then came the price.

"$100,000," Pinky said casually, as if discussing the weather.

Dunmore's eyes narrowed.

"That's rather steep old boy".

Pinky's grin didn't waiver.

"So's the terrain. And my guy flying you in? He's risking a lot. Non-negotiable...old boy".

The lord looked ready to argue, but Evelyn beat him to it.

"Pay the man".

Dunmore huffed but pulled out his wallet. A few minutes later, the transaction was done, and Pinky clapped his hands.

"Pleasure doing business," he said. "I'll have everything loaded up. You all better get some rest - you leave at first light to-morrow".

CHAPTER 4

DON'T LOOK NOW

The Cessna Caravan lifted off the pot holed airstrip just before dawn, its powerful turboprop engine roaring as it climbed into the sky. Below them, the dark waters of the Caribbean stretched out to the east, while the dense green of the Belizean jungle faded behind them.

Jake sat in the co-pilot's seat, scanning the instruments as their pilot - a grizzled ex-smuggler named Rees - adjusted their course. In the rear of the plane, the others dozed or watched the view through the small windows. Lecky stretched out with his arms behind his head, while Evelyn jotted down notes in her leather-bound journal.

Lord Dunmore, visibly uncomfortable, gripped the armrests as turbulence rocked the aircraft.

"Not a fan of flying?" Jake asked, amused.

"I prefer something larger. With a bar," Dunmore muttered.

Rees chuckled, chewing on an unlit cigar.

"This ain't the Ritz, but she'll get you where you need to go".

For hours, they flew south, crossing the vast expanse of Central America. Mountain ranges rose in the distance, then fell away to rivers snaking through the jungle below. The humid air shimmered on the horizon, the world beneath them an unbroken sea of green.

As they neared Peru, Rees cut the engine power slightly, lowering their altitude. The transition from open sky to jungle cloaked valleys was swift, and the sun had begun its descent by the time Rees pointed to a long, dirt airstrip barely visible between the trees.

Beyond it, the sprawling waterways of the Tambopata and Madre de Dios rivers shimmered in the fading light, winding their way past Puerto Maldonado - a frontier city carved from the wilderness. Even from the air, they could see the contrast between its bustling heart and the encroaching rainforest. Roads lined with motorcycles and market stalls gave way to an endless stretch of untamed jungle, where oxbow lakes and clay licks lay hidden beneath the dense canopy.

Rees guided the plane lower, the thick, humid air buffeting them as they descended. This was the gateway to the Amazon, where the past lingered in the ruins of the rubber boom, and the future was uncertain, shaped by gold miners, loggers, and those still daring enough to seek fortune in the depths of the rainforest.

"There's your landing spot. You sure about this?"

Jake nodded.

"No turning back now".

The twin-engine aircraft touched down on the rough jungle airstrip, its tyres kicking up a cloud of dust and leaves as the pilot fought the uneven ground, skidding to a halt at the far end of the overgrown runway. The landing was smoother than expected, though the thick canopy overhead made the strip feel more like a clearing hacked out of the wilderness than a proper runway. Rees taxied the Cessna to a stop near an abandoned wooden hangar, its tin roof rusted and partially collapsed.

As soon as the engines whined down, a lone figure emerged from the tree line - dark-skinned, dressed in a mix of military fatigues and local clothing, an old AK slung over one shoulder. He raised a hand in greeting.

Jake recognised the man instantly.

"That's Miguel. He's our contact".

Miguel gestured for them to move quickly. The group grabbed their gear whilst Jake pushed open the door, letting the heavy jungle air flood in. The scent of damp earth, rotting vegetation, and distant wood smoke filled his lungs, the oppressive humidity hitting them like a wall the moment they stepped off the plane.

Lecky tugged at his shirt collar, already sweating.

"It's like a goddamn sauna," he muttered.

Jake ignored the complaint, scanning the area. The airstrip consisted of little more than a dirt runway and the weathered wooden hangar standing near the tree line. A single Land Rover Defender sat waiting, faded green with dented panels and tyres caked in mud.

No one spoke much...everyone had the same instinct...get moving.

"Welcome to Peru," said Miguel, in Spanish-accented English, shaking Jake's hand.

His eyes flicked over the others, pausing briefly on Dunmore.

"I see you brought the gringo aristocrat?"

Lecky laughed.

"Ain't he just precious?"

Dunmore shot them a glare but said nothing.

Miguel smirked and gestured toward the tree line.

"Come. The Land Rover is waiting".

The supplies, weapons, and packs were loaded into the vehicle, and within minutes, they were rumbling down a narrow track that led away from the airstrip, the Cessna already taxiing back for its departure.

The jungle closed in around them as they left the airstrip behind, thick vegetation on both sides, vines and leaves brushing against the windows as the Land Rover bounced over deep ruts.

Lecky sat in the front with Miguel, while Jake, Evelyn, Tariq, and Dunmore squeezed into the back with their equipment.

"So where exactly are we headed?" Lecky asked, keeping his eyes on the jungle around them.

"Small town. A few hours from here. You sleep, eat, then move," Miguel replied.

Dunmore sighed.

"Finally, some bloody civilisation".

Jake snorted.

"Define 'civilisation'".

The drive took them through dense jungle that eventually gave way to rolling hills and scattered villages. By the time they reached the outskirts of the town of Cusco, dusk had settled, casting long shadows over the cracked streets.

The jungle road eventually gave way to crumbling asphalt as they neared the town - a mix of old Spanish-era buildings and ramshackle huts, where stray dogs roamed and market stalls lined the streets. It was the kind of place where everything was for sale, for the right price

Their hotel stood at the edge of the town square, a once grand building now faded by time and neglect. A wraparound balcony overlooked the square, where a few market stalls remained open under flickering lanterns. Inside, the reception area was dimly lit, its decor a mix of faded grandeur and local craftsmanship. A wooden ceiling fan spun lazily above the counter where a tired looking receptionist greeted them with polite disinterest, barely looking up as they checked in, and within minutes, they were upstairs in their rooms.

"A couple of hours to clean up, then we meet in the bar," Jake announced.

Lecky sighed, tossing his pack onto the bed.

"Finally, a goddamn shower".

With preparations nearly complete, Jake and Evelyn decided to explore the town on foot and perhaps have dinner at a restaurant not far from the hotel. They wandered through the bustling streets, taking in the scent of grilled meat and spices, the noise of street vendors calling out their wares, eventually finding a quiet restaurant with an open-air terrace. They selected a quiet spot in the corner, where candlelight flickered against the cracked plaster walls. The meal was simple but satisfying - grilled fish, rice, and fresh vegetables, accompanied by cold beer.

For the first time in days, there was a moment of calm.

"You realise we're never going to retire peacefully," Jake said, smiling as he clinked his beer against hers.

Evelyn smirked, taking a slow sip before replying.

"Speak for yourself. I fully intend to buy a vineyard and let someone else do all the work".

Jake chuckled, shaking his head.

"Yeah, right. You'd get bored in a week. You'd be out there with a clipboard, yelling at the workers about grape quality and optimum fermentation conditions".

Evelyn narrowed her eyes playfully.

"Excuse *me*; I am perfectly capable of lounging by a pool all day, sipping fine wine".

Jake snorted.

"Oh sure, for about a day. Then you'd start renovating the place, building a secret wine bunker, and hiring ex-military guards to protect your 'precious reserves'".

Evelyn gasped in mock offence.

"That actually sounds like a brilliant idea! And what about you? You'd last two weeks before you got bored and started looking for lost cause to champion".

Jake took a thoughtful sip of his beer.

"Hmm. Maybe. But if I was rich, I wouldn't work. I'd just live a great life...you can't take the money with you, so why not enjoy it?"

Evelyn tilted her head, studying him with a mischievous glint in her eyes.

"Enjoy it how, exactly?"

Jake grinned.

"Oh, you know...travelling the world, drinking good whisky, living in the moment".

He leaned in slightly.

"And maybe keeping a certain fiery archaeologist entertained".

Evelyn raised an eye brow.

"Entertained, huh?"

"Absolutely," Jake said, his voice dropping a little lower, "someone's gotta make sure you don't get too comfortable in that vineyard of yours".

Evelyn laughed softly, shaking her head.

"I swear, you're impossible".

Jake smiled.

"And yet, here you are, still stuck with me".

Evelyn rolled her eyes but smiled, clinking her glass against his again.

"To never retiring peacefully".

Jake grinned.

"To always keeping life interesting".

Their eyes met for a moment, and in that unspoken exchange, they both knew – they wouldn't trade this life for anything. The danger, the excitement, the thrill of the chase - it was who they were. A quiet retirement might sound appealing in theory, but deep down, neither of them could imagine a life without adventure, without the rush of the unknown.

And maybe, just maybe, they knew something else too. That no matter where this path led them - through jungles, lost cities, gunfights, or ancient secrets – they had each other.

After dinner, they strolled back toward the hotel. The streets were quieter now, mostly empty, the market stalls shut, and only a few vendors lingering under dim streetlights. The night air was alive with the distant buzz of insects. But something seemed off. Jake felt it. A presence.

Jake slowed his pace. He didn't turn his head, didn't stop walking, but the instinct was there - the unmistakable awareness of being followed.

"Keep walking," Jake murmured, "we've got company".

Evelyn nodded, gripping the Browning pistol concealed under her jacket.

"How many?"

Jake glanced at a shop window, catching a reflection in the glass. A man in dark clothing followed at a steady distance, his silhouette only just visible in the dim glow of street lamps.

"One. Black jacket".

Evelyn's expression didn't change.

"Alley up ahead".

They turned a corner into a narrow side street, and then ducked into the shadows, pressing against the brick wall. The footsteps hesitated at the entrance. Then they resumed.

As the man stepped into the alley's entrance, he was met with the full force of Jake's fist square between the eyes. The man staggered but stayed on his feet, blinking in surprise. Jake followed up with a powerful right hook, sending him sprawling onto the cobblestones. Evelyn moved in, kicking away the pistol that had slipped from the man's grip.

Before he could recover, Evelyn had her weapon in her hand, and Jake crouched down, pressing his knee against the man's chest.

"Who sent you?" Jake growled.

The man grinned through bloodied teeth.

"You know who".

Jake pulled out his knife, the blade glinting in the moonlight, twirling it lazily before pressing the tip lightly against the man's crotch.

"Yeah? Well, I like specifics".

The man laughed.

"You cannot run forever".

Jake frowned.

"Run? Do you want to rethink that answer?"

The man's grin faltered, a flicker of fear crossing his face before he exhaled sharply.

"The Crescent Templars," he spat, "they want to know where you've hidden the Book of Truth".

Jake and Evelyn exchanged a glance. They had barely escaped with their lives, from Afghanistan, with the book, and now the Templars were hunting for it.

Jake pressed the blade closer.

"Who else knows we're here?"

The man chuckled.

"You have no idea who you're up against."

Jake sighed.

"Wrong answer".

He shifted the knife just enough to make the man sweat.

"Alright! Alright!" the man gasped. "They know you came here, and they know what you seek".

Jake pressed the blade slightly harder.

"How?"

The man smirked.

"You're not the only ones hunting".

Evelyn's stomach tightened.

"Who else?"

The man laughed a morbid laugh, but didn't answer. Jake sighed, then knocked him unconscious with a final punch.

"Well, that was subtle," Evelyn muttered.

Jake smirked.

"Yeah, I should work on my charm".

Evelyn rolled her eyes.

"Oh well, at least we know who's following us now".

Jake retrieved the pistol and any cash the man had, tossing the ID card to Evelyn. It was fake. No surprise.

They stepped out of the alley, back onto the quiet street, leaving their pursuer to the *other* rats that lurked in the darkness.

Jake cursed under his breath.

"What's wrong Jake?" Evelyn enquired.

"I can't believe we just did that?" he replied.

"Did what?" asked Evelyn.

"Ducked into a dark alley. Whenever I see it done in films or on TV I'm always calling them idiots for getting themselves trapped...and now I'm just as bad," Jake replied.

"Well they're not *you* are they? And besides, we need to tell the others," Evelyn said.

Jake nodded his agreement.

"And we need to move...fast".

The Crescent Templars were close. But now, someone else was in the game too.

They moved quickly but without drawing attention, keeping their pace casual as they wove through the quiet streets back toward the hotel. Jake's hand brushed against Evelyn's, a silent reminder that they were in this together.

As they reached the lobby, the warm glow of the chandeliers did little to shake the tension settling in their bones. The others were waiting in the lounge - Lecky, Tariq, and Dunmore - all nursing drinks. Lecky leaned back in his chair, boots crossed at the ankles, but as soon as he caught sight of their expressions, he sat forward, eyes narrowing.

"What the hell happened to you two?" he asked, setting his drink down.

Jake tossed the fake ID onto the table.

"We had a visitor".

Lecky picked it up, squinting, and twirled the fake ID between his fingers.

"He's an ugly spud aint he?" he said with a smile, "and I assume from the dried blood on your knuckles that he didn't exactly invite you out for a friendly chat?"

Evelyn exhaled.

"Crescent Templars. They know we're here, and they know what we're looking for".

That got everyone's attention. Dunmore muttered a curse under his breath, while Tariq rubbed his jaw thoughtfully.

Lecky, however, just grinned.

"Ah, those sneaky bastards. You ever get tired of having secret cults after you, Jake?"

Jake smirked.

"Keeps things interesting".

Jake pondered for a moment.

"I bet you don't even know who they are *do* you?"

Lecky smiled and shrugged.

"Not a clue".

Jake exhaled and leaned back, but before he could speak Evelyn got there first.

"The Crescent Templars are a multi-faith organisation, made up of people who believe they're the rightful guardians of history's greatest secrets. They're an ancient order - part zealots, part warlords, part very well-funded lunatics. They date back centuries, supposedly linked to secret societies that have influenced history from the shadows, operating like ghosts - pulling strings in politics, funding conflicts. They don't care about religion so much as controlling knowledge - deciding what should be revealed and what should stay buried".

Jake nodded.

"And right now, they're after one thing - the Book of Truth".

Lecky's expression darkened.

"I thought after Afghanistan, they'd have bigger problems to deal with".

Evelyn shook her head.

"They never let things go. You know that".

Dunmore crossed his arms.

"The Book of Truth?"

"It's an alternative to all religious teachings. The *real* word of God...in a nutshell...and they know I have a copy," said Evelyn.

That got everyone's attention. Tariq straightened, and Dunmore swore under his breath.

Lecky's grin faded.

"They know?"

Evelyn's voice was steady.

"They don't believe it's out of our hands. They think we hid it, and as long as they believe that, they won't stop coming".

Tariq rubbed his jaw thoughtfully.

"But why the sudden interest now? We are not *here* for the book. We are seeking the Incan treasure and that supposed power source".

Jake drummed his fingers on the table.

"That's the real question. Either they think the treasure and the book are connected, or they just don't like the idea of us digging up something they haven't sanctioned".

Lecky exhaled.

"So, same old story...us looking for something valuable, them trying to make sure we never find it".

Jake smirked.

"You've hit the nail on the head mate".

Evelyn nodded.

"In any case, the Government locked the five physical copies away, so I e-mailed a scanned copy of mine to every major religious leader in the world".

There was silence for a moment.

"Did you hear back from any of them?" asked Lecky.

"Nope...not a sausage. I gave them a choice. Change religion, make the world better - or I go public. No more blind faith, no more corruption, no more using ancient words to justify war, hate, and greed".

Dunmore let out a low sigh.

"Very noble, I'm sure Miss Kane, but let me guess - the Templars, and no doubt the various faiths, really don't want that to happen".

Evelyn smirked.

"Not even a little".

Lecky sat back, arms folded.

"So, what's stopping you? If you want the world to know, just drop it to the press".

Evelyn's expression hardened.

"Because it has to mean something. If I just throw it out there, it'll be dismissed, buried, twisted. But if I can push the right people into action first...if religion chooses to change, even just a little, then maybe...maybe...it'll stick".

Lecky watched her for a long moment, then sighed.

"Well, that explains why they're after us".

Jake chuckled.

"You're catching on fast my friend".

"So, you are positive that they think you two still have it?" Dunmore asked.

Jake's grin faded.

"That's what our 'friend' in the alley seemed to think. But the book's long gone. It's locked away somewhere safe. The problem is, they don't believe that, or even care. They just want it".

"Great. So, they're hounding us for a book we don't even have, while we're trying to track down an Incan treasure and some mysterious power source?" said Lecky.

Jake nodded.

"That about sums it up".

Lecky sighed.

"You really know how to pick 'em, bud".

Jake smirked.

"I like to keep things interesting".

"And now there's someone else after us, which means the stakes just got higher," said Tariq.

Evelyn's voice was quiet but firm.

"In the end we need to find that treasure before anyone else does. If the Templars get to it first, or whoever else is in play, we might be dealing with something far worse than just another secret society".

Silence hung over the table for a moment. Then, Lecky let out a sigh.

"Well, that's lovely. And here I thought we were just in it for the gold".

A cheeky grin appeared on Jake's face.

"Who said we weren't?"

Lecky chuckled.

"Yeah? We just put a gun to the head of every major belief system on the planet, so it aint gonna be no walk in the park".

Evelyn shrugged.

"With all of the hate they are causing now, and *have* caused in the past, they had it coming".

Jake smirked.

"Remind me never to get on *your* bad side."

Lecky drained the rest of his drink and set the glass down with a thud.

"Alright, well, seeing as we're now enemies of every secretive, power hungry bastard in the world, I'm assuming we have a plan?"

Jake nodded.

"We need to stay ahead of them, and find out who else is in the game".

Tariq sighed.

"And I was hoping for an easy job..."

Jake grinned.

"Mate, you signed up with the wrong people for that".

Lecky stretched, cracking his neck.

"So, what are we doing? Running, or standing our ground?"

Jake ran a hand through his hair.

"Neither. We're moving out first thing. But there's more - our bloke in the alley wasn't just talking about the Templars. Someone else is in play".

Tariq's expression darkened.

"Someone who knows exactly what we are looking for I assume?"

"Well, he didn't go into specifics," replied Jake, "not with my fist in his face and knife up against his balls anyway".

Lecky muttered a curse under his breath.

"So, we've got the Templars breathing down our necks, and now a mystery player in the mix?"

Jake held his glass up towards Lecky and slightly bowed his head.

"Welcome to the party".

Lecky shook his head with a grin.

"You really are allergic to a quiet life".

Evelyn smirked.

"And *you* keep signing up for it".

Lecky chuckled.

"Yeah, well. Someone's got to keep you two out of trouble".

Dunmore was obviously annoyed, and didn't hold back.

"Damn it, I was hoping this would be a clean operation, and now we have this damn book and some other treasure hunter in play".

Lecky laughed.

"With Jake involved? Clean? Buddy, you should've known better".

Jake ignored him and leaned forward.

"We have no idea who else is involved, so we need to be careful. We'll load up and make tracks at dawn".

Evelyn glanced at Jake.

"Do you think our friend in the alley was the only one watching us?"

Jake shook his head.

"Not a chance".

Lecky chuckled.

"Well, I suppose there's no point in trying to get a good night's sleep, then".

Jake smirked.

"Who said we ever sleep?"

Evelyn rolled her eyes, but there was a flicker of amusement in them.

"Just try not to get shot before breakfast".

Jake winked.

"I'll do my best".

The group finished their drinks, the weight of the conversation settling over them like a storm about to break. Tomorrow, the trek into the unknown would begin.

CHAPTER 5

THE ANDES AWAIT

The sun had barely begun its climb over the Peruvian horizon when the team moved out. The streets of Cusco were still waking, shopkeepers setting up their stalls, the smell of fresh bread and coffee wafting through the air. The team moved through the city with purpose, their bags packed and ready for the trek ahead.

"So, just to be clear, we're walking straight into the jungle *knowing* that a bunch of religious fanatics want us dead?" Lecky asked.

Jake smirked.

"Yep".

Lecky sighed.

"Good. Wouldn't want to break tradition".

"I don't think they want us dead," Evelyn added, "I think they just want to possess all of the books".

"And *then* kill us..." said Jake.

Dunmore gazed at Evelyn.

"*All* of the books? Is there more than one out there?"

Tariq and Jake, who possessed the other two, cast a quick glance towards the ground. Their expressions couldn't have been guiltier if they had tried.

Dunmore shook his head.

"Bloody marvellous!"

He paused for a moment, the devious cogs turning in his head.

"So, there are three actual books as well as digitised ones...correct?"

Lecky laughed and looked over to Jake.

"He catches on fast eh?"

"And if there were?" Jake asked, a veil of wariness covering him.

"Well...they alone could be priceless...written by the hand of God and all that," replied Dunmore.

Jake was now feeling annoyed and trying to find a way out of the conversation.

"So? What's your point?"

"Sell them dear boy and you'll *never* have to work again," Dunmore answered, "where have you hidden them?"

Tariq cast a worried gaze towards Jake, and shook his head. Jake replied with a slight nod and held up his hand.

"You're having a laugh if you think I'm going to tell *you*. Let's just say that they are safe for now; that's all that matters".

"That makes it easier for these Templar fellows then doesn't it? You've squirreled them away to...who knows where...so get rid of you and their problem is solved," said Dunmore.

Dunmore was right. A sobering thought to the rest of the team indeed.

They reached their vehicle - a rugged, mud-splattered Land Rover waiting at the edge of town. Tariq climbed into the driver's seat and drummed his fingers on the wheel.

"If we are lucky, we will be deep into the mountains before anyone realises we have left".

Jake gave a dry chuckle.

"Luck hasn't exactly been on our side lately though has it?"

As they loaded their equipment into the back, Evelyn glanced around, her instincts prickling. Something was off.

She nudged Jake.

"We're being watched".

Jake didn't react, just finished tying down a pack before answering under his breath.

"Where?"

"Second floor, green shutters".

Jake casually stretched and glanced up. A man stood in the window, partially obscured by the curtain. The moment Jake's gaze met his, the figure disappeared from view.

Evelyn breathed out heavily.

"That wasn't a Templar".

Jake nodded grimly.

"No, it wasn't".

Dunmore frowned.

"Then who?"

Evelyn answered with a hesitant question.

"The other players in the game?"

Lecky swung into the passenger seat.

"Brilliant. So not only do we have the Crescent Templars breathing down our necks, but we've got mystery guests too".

Jake climbed into the backseat.

"Looks like it...got any enemies we don't know about your lordship?"

Dunmore spoke no more, but his face said it all.

As Tariq started the engine, the 4x4 rumbled to life, and they pulled onto the dirt road leading out of town. Dust kicked up in their wake, the city shrinking behind them.

Dunmore adjusted his hat and muttered, "I hate surprises".

Lecky turned in his seat, grinning.

"Then you're really gonna hate this trip".

Evelyn stared out the window, her mind racing. They were being hunted. Not just by the Templars, but by someone else - someone who had been watching, waiting, and whoever they were, they weren't far behind.

They rumbled out of town just after dawn, the golden light creeping over the terracotta rooftops as they left the city behind. The road was rough, winding through valleys and skirting the edges of towering mountains. The Land Rover jolted over potholes, the suspension groaning in protest as they climbed higher into the Andes. The morning mist still clung to the peaks, swirling like ghosts in the crisp air. The further they drove, the more civilisation faded - concrete buildings gave way to thatched huts, bustling markets to lonely stretches of road hugging the mountainside.

Evelyn watched the mist swirling around the peaks, and the scenery passing by; her mind troubled.

"I don't like how easy that was".

Tariq glanced at her in the rear view mirror.

"Easy?"

She nodded.

"No ambushes on the way back, no one following us this morning. Either the Templars are getting sloppy, or they want us to feel safe".

Jake rubbed his chin, tilting his hat forward over his eyes.

"Or they're letting us do the hard work for them. Why risk their own people when they can just wait for us to lead them to the prize?"

Lecky, who had been uncharacteristically quiet, finally spoke.

"Or maybe they're not the only ones we should be worried about".

Evelyn frowned.

"You're talking about the other players".

Dunmore, from the backseat, muttered, "Bloody wonderful".

"Yeah. The question is - who?" said Jake.

None of them had an answer.

But elsewhere, in the shadowed corners of the town, someone was already moving.

A man sat at a café terrace, sipping his morning coffee as he watched the distant trail of dust their vehicles left behind. He was dressed like any other traveller - hiking boots, cargo pants, a casual linen shirt - but his posture was too poised, his expression too knowing.

He reached into his pocket and pulled out a sleek satellite phone. He dialled a number and waited.

"They've left," he said simply when the call connected. A pause. Then he smiled a smug smile.

A voice on the other end of the line spoke, deep and measured. The man at the café listened, his smirk widening slightly.

"Yes. Let them go for now. We'll pick up their trail when they get closer".

He ended the call, pocketing the phone before tossing a few coins onto the table. Rising to his feet, he adjusted his sunglasses and strolled casually down the street, disappearing into the morning crowd.

Meanwhile, miles ahead, the team pushed deeper into the mountains. The roads turned from tarmac to dirt, and soon, even the dirt roads gave way to little more than winding tracks through dense jungle. The high altitude air was thin, but carried a weight - something unseen pressing down on them.

"Next town's another hour," Jake said, checking the GPS, "we'll stop there and get whatever local info we can".

Evelyn glanced at him.

"And after that?"

Jake thought for a moment before replying.

"Then we head into the unknown".

Lecky let out a low chuckle.

"You say that like we haven't been walking blind this whole time".

Evelyn settled back in her seat, watching the jungle blur past.

"There's blind...and then there's stepping off the edge of a cliff...anyway we have the old journal as a guide".

And somewhere far behind them, Richard Dunmore - the illegitimate older brother of Lord Dunmore - was already setting his own plans into motion. He had waited years for this moment, and he wasn't about to let his brother claim what he had knew should rightfully have been his.

The race for the lost Inca treasure - and the power hidden with it - had truly begun.

The dense jungle slowly gave way to rugged foothills, the road winding steadily upward into the towering Andes. The air grew cooler, the humidity of the lowlands replaced by the cool, thin atmosphere of higher elevations. Clouds clung to the mountainsides, swirling around sharp peaks like ghosts, while deep valleys yawned below, carved by rivers that had been cutting through the stone for centuries.

Waterfalls tumbled down sheer cliffs, their white torrents vanishing into the greenery far below. The narrow road twisted along the mountainside, hugging the edge in places where a single miscalculation would send them plunging into the valley far below.

The thick Amazonian vegetation had given way to a mix of cloud forest and cultivated land, where clusters of simple houses stood among small orchards of citrus and avocado trees.

The highway was mostly deserted, save for the occasional truck labouring up the incline or a motorbike weaving between potholes. Every so often, they passed through small villages, where adobe houses stood in clusters, their red-tiled roofs bright against the muted colours of the mountains.

Somewhere beyond the mist and peaks lay Machu Picchu, the famous Incan citadel perched high on its rocky throne. A thought lingered in the back of Jake's mind as he watched the landscape unfold around them.

"You know," he said, leaning back in his seat, "it'd be pretty funny if that monk was actually talking about Machu Picchu this whole time".

Evelyn shot him a look.

"The most famous lost city in the world?"

Jake grinned.

"Exactly. What if it was never really 'found' at all? Maybe we've all been looking at it the wrong way".

Evelyn snorted.

"Right. And next you'll tell me the Nazca Lines are just an ancient car park".

Jake shrugged.

"Hey, I don't even know what they are, but stranger things have happened".

The conversation died down as the road curved through another valley, the mountains closing in around them. After hours of driving, the group finally spotted their stop for the night - a small roadside inn nestled against the hillside, its faded sign reading Hostal Cañaveral.

As they pulled into the gravel car park, the group was met with an unexpected sight. Instead of the rustic, timeworn inn they had anticipated, Hostal Cañaveral stood sleek and modern against the backdrop of the Andes. A two storey, lime coloured building with a tiled roof, it featured a spacious patio, large glass windows, and a well maintained garden. A sign near the entrance boasted a restaurant, Wi-Fi, and - of all things - a swimming pool.

Lecky smiled a wide smile.

"Well, would you look at that? I was expecting a leaky shack with a donkey tied out front".

Tariq smiled as he shut off the engine.

"It is very good for the middle of nowhere".

Evelyn stepped out, stretching her legs. The air was noticeably cooler at this altitude, clean and fresh compared to the humid jungle they had left behind. A few guests, mainly backpackers, lounged by the pool, while others sat at outdoor tables, sipping coffee or beer.

Inside, the lobby was clean and inviting, with polished tile floors and walls adorned with local artwork. The restaurant smelled of grilled meat and fresh bread, making Jake's stomach growl loudly.

"Well," he said, rubbing his hands together, "I say we settle in, grab a meal, and enjoy this little slice of civilisation while we can".

Lecky raised an eyebrow.

"Feeling soft already?"

"Hey," Jake grinned, "just because we're chasing lost cities doesn't mean we can't enjoy a little luxury along the way. In our line of work it makes a pleasant change".

Evelyn chuckled.

"Let's just hope the beds are as nice as the rest of the place".

With that, they checked in, still slightly in disbelief at their unexpected good fortune.

The evening settled in with a warm, golden glow over the mountains, the clean Andean air carrying the faint scent of grilled meat and wood smoke from the outside kitchen. By the time they had freshened up and returned to the poolside, the sky had deepened to a rich indigo, the first stars appearing overhead.

Jake stretched out on a lounge chair, drink in hand, and sighed contentedly.

"You know," he said, lifting his glass of beer toward the others, "I think I could get used to this. Who knew searching for lost cities involved alcohol and a swimming pool?"

Lecky smirked, swirling the ice in his glass.

"Don't get too comfortable. Something tells me this is the last bit of luxury we'll see for a while".

Evelyn, cross-legged on a sun lounger, had the monk's journal spread open in her lap, her eyes scanning the delicate handwriting. A candlelit lantern on the table flickered, casting shifting shadows across the worn pages.

"Might as well enjoy it while we can," she murmured, running her finger along a passage, "I'm looking for anything obvious, you know...landmarks, something concrete".

A waiter appeared with steaming plates of lomo saltado, sizzling strips of beef with onions, tomatoes, and fried potatoes, along with fresh bread and a bowl of green ají sauce. The rich aroma was enough to pull Jake's attention away from the journal.

"Alright, hold that thought," he said, reaching for his knife and fork, "lost city or not, I need fuel".

Evelyn gave him an exasperated glance but relented, taking a sip of her chilcano cocktail before marking her place.

"Fine. But once we've eaten, we're going through this properly".

Jake grinned.

"Fine by me. Maybe the monk wrote, 'Head south until you hit a five star resort, then take a left at the jungle'".

"If only it were that easy," laughed Lecky.

As they dug into their meal, the journal sat between them, its secrets waiting to be uncovered.

After dinner, Evelyn sat at a shaded table, flipping through the monk's journal, her brow furrowed. Pages of meticulous, looping script described a journey through mountains and forests, but so far, no obvious clues.

"This thing reads like a damn riddle," she muttered. "'Through the green sea, past the tears of the mountain, where the stars meet the earth...' What is that even supposed to mean?"

Lecky leaned over, taking a sip of his drink.

"Could be poetry. Could be directions".

Jake smiled.

"It *could* be absolute nonsense".

Evelyn sighed and leaned back, scanning the surrounding mountains, their slopes veiled in wisps of mist.

"If it's real, we're looking in the wrong place. The Inca didn't build cities deep in the jungle. They built in the mountains, where they could control trade and keep an eye on their enemies."

"And yet," Jake said, flipping through the pages, "this monk seems to think they found something hidden lower down, further north".

He grinned.

"It would be funny if it really is Machu Picchu. That'd be a laugh eh?"

Evelyn rolled her eyes.

"Hilarious".

Dunmore snorted.

"Thousands of tourists walk through it every day. It's hardly a lost city".

Evelyn sat up suddenly.

"No, but Machu Picchu was forgotten for centuries before Hiram Bingham stumbled on it. If the Spanish missed that, what else could be out there?"

She ran a finger along the faded ink.

"The journal mentions an ancient path leading away from a known ruin...deeper into the mountains".

Jake raised an eyebrow.

"And let me guess...we just happen to be near that ruin?"

She nodded.

"If I'm right, we need to head north, along the old Inca trails. There aren't any rivers, just steep paths and cloud forests. But something's out there".

Lecky set his glass down.

"Then we'd better find a guide".

Jake grinned and lifted his drink.

"To finding lost cities".

Their glasses clinked together, the fading sunlight turning the Andean peaks into silhouettes against the burning sky.

The waiter, a young local named Mateo, lingered near their table, pretending to wipe down a tray. He had been listening - probably since they'd first mentioned lost cities.

"You are looking for something in the jungle senorita?" he asked hesitantly, glancing around as if to make sure no one else was listening.

"You *could* say that," said Jake, casting his eyes on the waiter.

Mateo hesitated, and then leaned forward.

"There is an old story. My grandfather told it to me when I was a boy," his voice dropped to a near whisper, "a city...hidden beneath the jungle, covered by time. And at night, it glows".

Evelyn's fingers tightened around the journal.

"Glows?"

Mateo nodded.

"Not many believe it. They say the city was abandoned long ago. Some think the jungle swallowed it. Others say it is cursed. They call it the city of shadows...but these shadows bring only death...or so I am told".

"So...the city of death then? Great!" said Jake.

Lecky raised an eyebrow.

"And you believe it?"

Mateo shrugged.

"I do not know. But I know this – north of here, beyond the mountains, there are places where no one goes," he gestured vaguely, "old trails, swallowed by the forest, and ancient peoples who know nothing of us, still living in the past. My grandfather said men went looking, but they never returned".

Jake leaned back in his chair, grinning.

"Well, that sounds promising," he said sarcastically.

Evelyn ignored him.

"Where exactly?"

Mateo paused, and then tapped the table.

"If you go north, past the old ruins, there is a valley. It is far – many days on foot. But some say strange lights can be seen in the distance on stormy nights," he straightened, "that is all I know".

Lecky exhaled.

"So we're going deep. No roads, no rivers...just trails".

Evelyn nodded and raised an eyebrow; a worried expression on her face.

Jake lifted his glass.

"Cheer up Evie, it may never happen".

The next morning, as they packed up their gear, Mateo lingered near the entrance of the hotel, shifting his weight from foot to foot. He looked like a man wrestling with an idea he didn't quite like.

"You're still thinking about that glowing city, aren't you?" Jake asked, tossing his pack into the truck.

Mateo glanced around, then sighed.

"It is a story. Probably just a legend".

Evelyn folded her arms.

"But *you* know the mountains? You know the old trails?"

Jake nodded his agreement.

"We need a guide, Mateo. Someone who won't get us lost out there".

Mateo hesitated.

"I have work here".

Jake grinned.

"I'm sure the Hostal will survive without you for a while".

Evelyn took a different approach.

"What if it's real? The lost city? You'd be the first person in centuries to see it...and we will pay you well. How does $200 a day sound?"

That got his attention. A flicker of something crossed his face - curiosity, or maybe something deeper.

"And if we don't find anything?"

Jake shrugged.

"Then you still get paid."

Mateo exhaled through his nose. Then, reluctantly, he nodded.

"Gracias. But I have conditions".

Jake paused and smiled.

"Aye, aye..."

Mateo held up a finger.

"First, we take no shortcuts. The jungle is dangerous. If we go off the trails, we could be lost forever".

A second finger.

"Second, we listen to the mountains. If the weather changes, we stop. If the jungle says 'go back,' we go back".

A third finger.

"And...er...how you say...en tercer lugar..."

He paused, then lowered his hand.

"We do not talk about this to anyone else".

Jake raised an eyebrow.

"Why? Are you afraid someone will steal our imaginary city?"

Mateo didn't smile.

"There are others who listen. And not all of them want the city to be found...at least not by you".

That got everyone's attention.

Lecky clapped a hand on Mateo's shoulder.

"Looks like we've got ourselves a guide".

The sun hung low as they left the last traces of civilisation behind, their Land Rover rumbling along a narrow dirt road that twisted through the foothills of the Andes. The land was wild and rugged, the slopes covered in dry scrub and tangled vegetation, with only the occasional crumbling stone wall hinting at the past.

The last town was little more than a scattering of whitewashed buildings, its narrow streets lined with fruit vendors and wandering dogs.

Mateo had led them out of town and onto a winding dirt road that snaked up through the foothills. The jungle thickened around them, the air growing hot, dense, and filled with the hum of unseen insects. As they climbed higher, the green walls of the rainforest closed in, towering ceibas and tangled vines swallowing the sky.

By mid-afternoon, the dirt road had turned into little more than a track, hemmed in by steep ridges and dense forest. The trees had grown taller, the air heavier, thick with the scent of damp earth and distant rain. They drove on, the engine straining as the road climbed higher into the mountains.

After hours of slow progress, Mateo signalled for them to stop. Ahead, the road had simply vanished - overgrown, swallowed by the jungle. A crumbling stone wall, half-buried under creeping moss, marked the remains of some forgotten outpost.

"This is as far as we drive," Mateo said, "from here, we walk".

Jake stretched, rolling his shoulders.

"Well, that's convenient. No way back but forward".

"How far?" Tariq enquired.

"Several days. Perhaps more. It depends on the trails".

Lecky paused for a moment, carefully scanning the trees.

"Anyone else feel like we're being watched?

The jungle was alive with noise - chattering insects, distant bird calls, the occasional rustle of unseen creatures. But there was something else too. A stillness beneath it all. A weight in the air.

"I do not think it is animals..." Mateo murmured.

No one argued, each exchanging glances. Something...someone...was out there. But for now whoever, or whatever, it was stayed in the shadows.

They secured the Land Rover, covering it with branches and loose foliage. Then, with packs on their backs and machetes in hand, they stepped into the unknown.

CHAPTER 6

GODS OF FIRE

The jungle quickly engulfed them, thick with vines and towering trees that tangled overhead, blocking out the sky. Every step forward was a battle. Tariq swung his machete, hacking through the dense vegetation, while Mateo followed close behind, clearing the path further. Sweat dripped down their faces, the humid air clinging to their skin like a second layer.

Overhead, flashes of colour flitted between the branches - parrots and macaws squawking loudly at the intruders below. A troop of monkeys shrieked and crashed through the canopy, their movements sending a shower of leaves to the jungle floor. Then, somewhere deeper in the trees, a low, husky growl rumbled through the air.

Lecky stopped mid-step.

"*That* wasn't a monkey".

"Jaguar," Mateo muttered, glancing toward the sound, "it's not close. But they are always watching".

Jake wiped sweat from his brow.

"Good to know".

He looked around for a moment.

"You know, this place takes me back to jungle training in Borneo. It's like a bloody greenhouse though".

Lecky chuckled.

"More like a green prison".

A sudden loud, high-pitched squeal broke the moment. A huge spider had suddenly dropped from a branch onto Dunmore's shoulder.

"GET IT OFF!" he yelped, his voice almost an octave higher than usual.

Evelyn, entirely unfazed, stepped forward and casually flicked the spider away with the back of her hand. The tarantula tumbled into the undergrowth and disappeared.

Dunmore gulped, visibly rattled, and clutched his chest, trying to regain his composure, but the others exchanged knowing looks, biting back grins.

Jake was the first to comment...witty as ever.

"Well, that was dignified".

Lecky nudged Jake, grinning.

"The man's a true explorer".

Jake leaned toward Lecky and whispered.

"Did he just shriek like a schoolgirl?"

Lecky smirked.

"He sure did".

Dunmore cleared his throat loudly, pretending nothing had happened.

"Come on...show's over...let's keep moving shall we?"

The jungle thinned at last, as they reached a clearing just before dusk, revealing a crumbling stone platform, half-swallowed by roots and moss. At its centre stood a weathered and ancient sun dial, its edges smoothed by centuries of exposure, and covered in deep engravings, vines snaking over its face.

Jake ran a hand across the markings.

"Think it still works?"

Lecky glanced up at the thick jungle canopy overhead, where no sunlight could penetrate.

"Probably did...before all this grew over the top".

Tariq knelt by the base, brushing away dirt and moss.

"There is something written here".

Evelyn crouched beside him, fingers tracing the faint glyphs.

"It's in Spanish...it says...*Turn back before the light fades. The path ahead is not for the living*".

"Charming...that's not ominous at all is it...hey, I didn't know you could speak Spanish," said Jake.

"How did you think I was reading the journal? Besides, I have many hidden talents you don't know about Jakey my boy," Evelyn replied with a cheeky smile.

Jake winked.

"I can't wait to find out".

Silence settled over the group.

"I think you two need to get a room..." said Lecky.

Dunmore coughed and shifted uncomfortably.

"It could just be superstition".

Mateo studied the stone.

"Or a warning".

A breeze rustled the trees around them. Somewhere a branch snapped.

Jake and Lecky clenched their weapons and nodded to Evelyn and Tariq.

"I think we'd better organise a watch for tonight...just in case," said Jake.

As the last of the daylight faded, the group set up camp in the clearing. It was a humid night and the scent of damp earth and crushed leaves was overpowering. Distant howls and strange animal calls echoed through the trees, a reminder that they were far from alone.

Lecky dropped his pack and stretched.

"Right guys, and lady, unless you fancy waking up covered in ants or worse, you'll want a shelter off the ground".

Jake nodded.

"First rule of jungle camping - never sleep on the floor if you can help it".

Tariq frowned.

"There is nothing but trees".

"Exactly," Lecky said, grabbing a length of sturdy vine, "this is where a little bushcraft comes in handy".

With Jake and Lecky leading the way, they used branches and vines to fashion small, makeshift platforms between the trees, just high enough to keep them out of reach of whatever might slither or scuttle in the night. Each shelter was covered with a waterproof army poncho, draped over the centre support to form a pitched roof above their heads. Mosquito nets were also incorporated, giving them an extra layer of protection against the swarming insects.

Dunmore examined his wobbly shelter, his face doubtful.

"You're telling me I'm meant to sleep on this?"

"Unless you'd rather cuddle up with a snake," Jake said, tossing him a spare length of string, "up to you".

Evelyn tested her own platform, surprisingly sturdy after a few adjustments.

"It'll do".

As they worked, packs were hung low on branches, keeping them out of reach of ground-dwelling creatures. The shelters were raised just enough to avoid sudden gushes of water from the frequent downpours and keep them safe from anything crawling around on the jungle floor.

Lecky dug into his pack and pulled out a spare pair of socks.

"One more thing – if you're gonna take your boots off, always put a sock in each boot overnight".

Dunmore raised an eyebrow.

"Why?"

Lecky smirked.

"Because if you don't, you might find a scorpion, a centipede, or some other nightmare curled up in there by morning".

Dunmore visibly tensed.

"You're joking".

Jake gave him a sarcastic look.

"Is he laughing...and besides, do you want to take that risk?"

With a grumbled curse, Dunmore shoved his socks into his boots.

A small fire flickered in the centre of camp, its glow barely piercing the shadows of the jungle. As they settled in, the sounds of the night intensified - the rustling of unseen creatures, the distant growl of a predator, and the constant buzzing of insects.

Evelyn exhaled, looking up at the dark canopy above.

"It feels like the jungle is watching us".

Lecky threw another stick on the fire.

"That's because it is".

For the next few days, they hacked their way through the never ending vegetation, their boots sinking into damp earth, their bodies drenched in sweat. With every breath that they took they inhaled the odour of damp leaves and decaying wood, whilst the sounds of the jungle echoed all around them.

Dunmore, his once neat attire now sweat-streaked and tattered, stumbled, for what felt like the hundredth time, cursing under his breath.

"Bloody nightmare," he muttered, swatting at a mosquito the size of his thumb, "this is no place for civilised men".

Jake, leading the group with his machete, didn't even glance back.

"Good thing there's none of those here, then".

"There *is* a civilised woman though," Evelyn quipped.

Jake turned to look at her and smiled.

"I wouldn't go *that* far".

"Cheeky bugger," laughed Evelyn.

Lecky grinned, nudging Jake.

"Do you reckon Dunmore quit Sandhurst or got booted?"

Jake didn't hesitate.

"Oh, he quit alright. There's no way that the instructors would let someone like him past the first week".

Dunmore huffed indignantly, pushing his way forward.

"I'll have you know..."

His foot caught on a root before he could finish his sentence, and he pitched forward, landing face first in the mud".

Lecky laughed.

"I rest my case..."

Jake winced.

"I bet that hurt".

Evelyn sighed, shaking her head.

"If he breaks his neck, *I'm* not carrying him".

Jake laughed.

"If he breaks his neck the only thing we'll be doing is digging a grave for him".

Lecky pulled Dunmore to his feet, brushing him off with minimal patience.

"Come on, Lord Complains-a-lot, let's get a move on".

"I *am* funding this expedition don't forget," growled Dunmore.

Jake paused and pointed to the jungle ahead of them.

"Be my guest".

Dunmore said nothing.

The first sign of human presence came when they stumbled upon a series of stone totems, half-buried in the undergrowth. The figures were worn by time, their faces elongated and eerie, carved with expressions of reverence or fear.

Evelyn ran her fingers over the moss-covered surface.

"These aren't Incan".

"Older?" asked Tariq.

She nodded.

"Much older".

A rustling in the undergrowth made them all freeze.

Jake brought his rifle into the aim, making a quick scan of the jungle. Lecky did the same. Dunmore, however, was too pre-occupied with his boots, pouring out liquid mud and flicking off leeches to notice the figures emerging from the foliage.

A dozen men, naked, apart from a loin cloth, and painted with ochre and black, stepped into view, their bows drawn, spears levelled.

Evelyn swore under her breath.

"And here I was hoping for a warm welcome and an uneventful expedition".

The tension was immediate - both groups staring at each other across the clearing, weapons raised. The leader of the warriors, an older man draped in feathers and beads, studied them with piercing eyes. His gaze lingered on Evelyn before he spoke in a language none of them understood.

Tariq lowered his weapon first, stepping forward with open hands. He touched his chest, then pointed at the ground, a universal sign of peace...but perhaps not so universal in the Peruvian jungle.

The chief narrowed his eyes, then spoke again. The warriors did not lower their weapons.

As Evelyn's eyes darted over the group, she suddenly froze. One of the warriors, standing off to the side, was dressed differently to the others, his chest bearing an unmistakable rusted steel breastplate. Even more jarring, atop his head sat a corroded conquistador's helmet, its once-polished surface dulled by centuries of jungle decay.

She gasped uncontrollably then cast a look towards the others.

"Look..."

As Dunmore clapped eyes on the armour clad warrior his mind went straight to money.

"If those are real there is a fortune adorning that chap over there...perhaps we can talk him out of them?"

Evelyn ignored the remark. The sight sent a chill through her. This wasn't some replica or decoration – this was real. But the question was, had it been passed down through generations? Was this proof that the Spanish had reached deeper into the jungle than history recorded?

She opened her mouth to say something, but thought better of it. Now wasn't the time to start asking questions.

Thinking fast, she dug into her pack and pulled out a metal prismatic compass, flicking it open to show the moving needle. She held it up for the chief to see, silently hoping that curiosity would override hostility.

He raised an eyebrow, then took a step closer, hesitantly reaching out.

Evelyn turned it in her hand, letting him see that it moved. The chief's eyes widened. He spoke rapidly to his warriors, and one of the younger men broke away, disappearing into the jungle.

"I think that did something," Tariq muttered.

Dunmore sniffed.

"Or he is fetching reinforcements to kill us?"

Jake elbowed him sharply.

"You're not helping Alex".

Minutes passed before the young warrior returned, carrying something wrapped in woven cloth. The chief unwrapped it carefully, revealing a metal disk covered in strange engravings. The edges were jagged, broken, as if it had once been part of a larger whole. He offered it to Evelyn.

Her breath caught.

"That looks like..."

Tariq finished for her.

"A piece of an astrolabe".

Lecky scratched his head.

"Now, I aint college educated, but I aint dumb either, but can someone tell me what the hell an astrolabe is please?"

Evelyn adjusted the brass instrument in her hands, turning it slightly so the filigree-cut metal plate caught the light.

"This," she said, offering it to Lecky, "is an astrolabe. Think of it as a star map and a calculator rolled into one".

Lecky took it, frowning at the intricate markings and movable parts.

"Looks more like a fancy bit of clockwork to me".

Evelyn chuckled.

"I suppose it does, but it's far older than any clock. The Greeks had them, the Arabs perfected them, and medieval sailors and scholars relied on them. It can measure how high a star or the sun is above the horizon, helping you figure out where you are - your latitude, at least. You can use it to tell time, identify stars, even survey land".

Lecky turned it over in his hands.

"And people actually used these instead of just looking at the sky and guessing?"

"Well, guessing isn't terribly precise, is it?" she said. "It was especially useful for astronomers and navigators, though at sea, the waves made it tricky. That's why they later developed the sextant".

She tapped the edge of the astrolabe with a knowing smile.

"But on solid ground, this little beauty was indispensable".

The chief snatched back the astrolabe and held it up, speaking urgently. He pointed at the engraved symbols, then at the jungle. Finally, he mimicked flickering lights with his fingers..

"I think he may be talking about the city which you seek," said Mateo.

Lecky gestured to the warriors' painted skin, noticing a symbol repeated on several of them – a crescent shape with rays extending from it, like a sun trapped in darkness.

"They definitely know something," Lecky murmured.

The chief, seemingly satisfied that they understood, took a step forward and gestured for them to follow him. His warriors fanned out to make a path for the group to follow.

Lecky looked over to Jake.

"What do you think buddy?"

Evelyn spoke before Jake had time to respond.

"I think we should go with them. They seem friendly enough".

"Said the spider to the fly," replied Jake.

Dunmore seemed visibly shaken.

"They might be cannibals".

"Hopefully they'll eat you first then," Jake mumbled under his breath.

"I *can hear* you, you know!" Dunmore responded.

"Good to know you are good at something," Jake quipped.

Lecky let out a sharp sigh.

"Well, we've come this far. Might as well see where they're taking us".

Jake shot him a dubious look but fell into step as the group moved forward, flanked by the silent warriors. The jungle pressed in thick on either side, the dimming light making the towering trees seem even more foreboding. Somewhere in the distance, a howler monkey let out a guttural cry, answered by another deeper in the undergrowth.

Evelyn walked beside the chief, watching as he occasionally glanced at the astrolabe. Every so often, he would point toward the dense foliage or the sky, muttering to himself.

"You reckon he's using it?" Jake asked in a low voice, nodding toward the device in the chief's hand.

"If he is, it means he understands it better than we do," Evelyn replied.

After nearly an hour of winding through narrow trails and wading across a shallow, pebbled stream, the jungle suddenly gave way to a clearing. The village was built in a natural basin, the huts made of tightly woven fronds and wood, their roofs sloping steeply to channel the rainfall. A massive central fire burned in the heart of the settlement, the smoke curling lazily into the evening sky.

Children peered at them from behind woven screens, while the elders sat cross-legged near the fire. As the chief led them toward the centre of the village, a group of women appeared, carrying wooden bowls filled with roasted meat, tubers, and a dark, steaming broth. The chief studied them warily, then gestured for them to sit by the fire.

Jake and Lecky exchanged glances, then cautiously followed. Dunmore hesitated, whilst Evelyn and Tariq sat without a thought, sensing that this was an invitation rather than an ultimatum.

Lecky paused as a bowl was pressed into his hands.

"Well, if they were going to kill us, they probably wouldn't bother feeding us first," he muttered.

Jake sniffed at his portion, then took a cautious bite.

"Not bad," he admitted, "but they *could* just be fattening us up".

Evelyn sat beside Lecky, her eyes flicking to the chief. He was speaking with an older man, gesturing toward the astrolabe again. The elder nodded, then traced a shape into the dirt at his feet - a circle with rays stretching outward, matching the markings on the warriors' skin.

Evelyn nudged Lecky.

"Look at that".

Lecky swallowed his mouthful of food and leaned forward, studying the drawing. The elder pointed at it, then toward the jungle, speaking in a hushed, urgent tone.

The warriors began to murmur amongst themselves as the chief reached into a woven pouch at his waist and pulled out a smooth, black stone disk, etched with symbols. It gleamed in the firelight, and was similar to the broken astrolabe.

Evelyn leaned forward, her eyes fixed on the disk as the chief turned it slowly in his hands. The intricate carvings caught the firelight, revealing symbols that looked eerily similar to the ones they had seen on the ancient sundial.

Jake reached for a stick and, just like the elder, began tracing a rough sketch in the dirt - a simple sun, then a city with high walls. He pointed to the sky, then back to the drawing, mimicking the motion of the sun rising and setting.

Mateo was becoming frustrated. How could he guide them if no one, not even himself, could understand the natives?

"I wish they could speak English or español!" he blurted out.

The chief's eyes lit up at the word. He stepped forward, a cautious smile creeping across his weathered face.

"Español? Si".

"Hablas español" Mateo asked.

The chief nodded slowly, as if reaching back through generations.

"Poco...de los antiguos".

Mateo blinked, then looked to the others.

"He says...he speaks a little Spanish, from the ancients".

Evelyn stepped closer, her eyes narrowing.

"He said the old ones. That must be how his people learned it. The conquistadors".

Conquistadors...the chief seemed to recognise the word, but said nothing.

Tariq folded his arms.

"That makes sense. If their ancestors had contact with the Spanish centuries ago, the language could have survived - bits and pieces passed down".

Jake nodded his agreement.

"His ancestors must have met the Spanish when they came through here".

Mateo turned back to the chief, his voice steadier now.

"I will ask him about the city...podemos hablar...sobre la ciudad?"

The chief gave a solemn nod and pointed again to the astrolabe - then to the jungle beyond - and barked a sharp command to the warriors.

They murmured, shifting uneasily. His sharp eyes flicked from Jake to Evelyn, his brow furrowed as if weighing something, then he jabbed a gnarled finger at the sun in Jake's drawing, then dragged it downward - not in a natural arc, but straight into the earth.

Evelyn stretched her neck as she leaned forward.

"Down? He's saying its underground?"

The chief didn't speak. Instead, he tapped the stone disk twice against his chest. Then, in broken, accented Spanish, he rasped, "Muchos...antes..."

He paused, searching for the word.

"Padres".

Mateo translated.

"Missionaries".

Evelyn's expression darkened.

"They *were* here".

The chief gave a solemn nod, then reached out and smudged Jake's drawing, wiping away the carefully drawn city walls with his palm. In their place, he drew jagged lines - mountains, or perhaps canyons - deep grooves that twisted across the ground. Then he tapped his chest again.

"Mi padre...abuelo...vieron".

Mateo swallowed hard, his heart thudding.

"He says his grandfather saw it".

They all stared down at the new drawing. Evelyn glanced at Jake.

"If the city *is* real...it's buried. Hidden somewhere in the jungle".

"And by the sound of it we're not the first to come looking".

Dunmore, who had been shifting uncomfortably, scoffed.

"Marvellous. Now we're chasing ghost stories!"

Before anyone could respond, the chief lifted a hand to silence them, then murmured something else.

"He says the city is real, and that it still watches the sky," said Mateo.

A shiver ran down Evelyn's spine.

"What does that mean?"

Mateo frowned.

"I do not know senorita but I think we are about to find out".

The chief pointed towards the mountains in the distance, then held up two fingers before crossing his arms in an X over his chest.

Mateo translated softly.

"I think that means two days journey".

But it was the crossed arms that made Evelyn uneasy. She glanced at Mateo.

"That means danger, doesn't it?"

Mateo exhaled.

"Si".

A gust of wind stirred the flames, casting wild shadows over the gathered figures. Somewhere beyond the village, a low, fearsome growl rumbled in the night. The jungle was listening...and it was waiting.

Jake barely had time to decipher the chief's warning before the old man suddenly turned his gaze to Evelyn. His eyes twinkled with something other than wisdom now - something far more mischievous.

The chief tapped his chest, then pointed at Evelyn.

"Mujer".

Mateo shifted awkwardly, swatting a mosquito that had settled on his forearm.

"Uh...he is offering marriage".

There was a momentary silence, which was broken by Jake.

"Marriage...tell him to bugger off mate!"

Evelyn blinked.

"Excuse me?"

Dunmore snorted.

"Congratulations Miss Kane...you're engaged".

The warriors laughed amongst themselves, clearly amused. Two of them stepped forward, gesturing toward Evelyn as if inviting her to join them. Their grins weren't exactly reassuring.

The chief mimed a wedding, complete with a bartering gesture.

"I think he is offering a trade...Miss Kane for safe passage," said Mateo.

Jake took a pace forward, his tone dry.

"Not happening mate".

Evelyn folded her arms, lifting a brow.

"Tell him I'm flattered, but I'm already spoken for".

Jake eyes widened.

"Oh yeah? Who's the lucky bloke?"

Evelyn turned to Jake and poked her tongue out.

Despite the tension, the team couldn't help but chuckle. Even the chief looked briefly puzzled by the exchange, then puckered his lips and made a series of exaggerated kissing noises, prompting a round of laughter from his warriors.

Lecky nudged Jake.

"Go on, buddy. It might be worth it for a shortcut".

Jake smirked.

"Nah, she's too much trouble. We'd just end up rescuing her anyway".

"It'd probably be the chief who'd need rescuing," replied Lecky.

"Hey! Cheeky buggers," Evelyn protested, "you'd be lost without me".

As Mateo nervously relayed the response, the chief frowned, clearly not expecting rejection. The joking quickly stopped when the chief barked another order. The warriors stopped laughing. Two stepped closer to Evelyn.

Jake sighed.

"Right. Time for a demonstration".

He pulled a lighter from his pocket and flicked it open. A tiny flame danced in the air. The nearest warriors froze, eyes staring at the apparently magic flame. A hush fell.

Then Evelyn, without missing a beat, grabbed a flare from her pack, struck it against a rock, and sent a blinding red glow hissing into the sky.

The response was immediate.

Warriors stumbled back, some dropping to their knees, hands raised in awe or fear. The chief's mouth fell open. He backed up a step, visibly rattled.

"Well, that worked," said Dunmore.

The chief recovered quickly, shouting an order. His men lowered their weapons and stepped aside, parting like a curtain.

Evelyn turned to Jake, eyes glittering.

"So...what now, fire god?"

Jake smirked.

"Let's just say I don't share".

As they began moving, the chief gave one final, theatrical sigh. He pointed at Evelyn, then at Jake, and shook his head in mock disappointment, muttering something in Spanish.

Mateo translated.

"He says you'll change your mind when you get tired of these fools".

Evelyn laughed.

"It's a bit late for that!"

"Come on...before he throws in a few goats," Jake said.

With one last glance at the flickering fire and the wary, wide-eyed faces of the villagers, the team stepped into the jungle once more.

Behind them, the chief watched in silence, his expression stern. Jake looked back, just once.

"Something tells me we haven't seen the last of them," he thought to himself.

CHAPTER 7

JUSTICE

The jungle was dense, a never ending tangle of vines and towering trees, making every step a challenge. The humidity clung to them like a second skin, and the air was alive with the sound of cicadas, squawking parrots, and the occasional rustling in the undergrowth.

Jake slung his pack off his shoulders and wiped a hand across his brow.

"I'd sell my soul for a cold beer".

"Make that two," Evelyn muttered, pulling her canteen from her belt and taking a swig.

They had found a small clearing, just large enough to stretch out and construct a camp site for the night. The trees around them were ancient, their gnarled roots weaving through the earth like snakes, but they were perfect for their shelters.

Night had settled over the camp like a heavy curtain. The rain had eased to a light drizzle, but the canopy above still wept fat droplets onto the leaf-littered ground. They kept a fire going low and small, casting faint, shifting light across their tired faces.

They set a sentry rota - two-hour shifts. With the jungle around them so close, none of them were taking chances.

Jake stretched out under his poncho, boots still on, rifle by his side, the sling coiled around his hand. He gave Dunmore a weary nod.

"Give me a shake when it's my turn," he mumbled, then slipped into a restless sleep.

The night passed in a blur of shifting shadows and jungle noises. Nothing out of the ordinary. No alarms. No raised voices.

It wasn't until the first light of dawn pushed through the trees that Jake stirred again. He rubbed his eyes, then glanced around, frowning.

"Dunmore?" he called out. "Dunmore, you lazy sod - you didn't wake me for my stag".

There was no answer. Dunmore was slumped by the fire, fast asleep, his chin resting on his chest.

Lecky suddenly woke and clambered out of his shelter, stretching a crick out of his back.

"I thought you had the last watch".

"I did!" Jake snapped, "or I was supposed to - bloody hell!"
He kicked Dunmore's boot.

"Oy! You were supposed to wake me!"

Dunmore jolted awake, blinking in confusion.

"I...I must have...just nodded off for a bit".

"A bit?" Jake growled. "It's a good job this isn't a war zone...*and* we have a woman here don't forget!"

"Ha! Evelyn can look after herself," Lecky laughed, as he turned his head towards her shelter, "wait...where is she?"

They rushed over.

Her pack was still there. So was her canteen. But the shelter was empty.

Jake crouched down, scanning the mud. His voice dropped low.

"There...look".

Bare footprints...a dozen maybe. Small and narrow, pressed deep into the wet ground around her shelter, and leading off into the jungle.

The realisation hit like a punch in the guts.

Jake scowled.

"She's been taken..."

Lecky, now fully alert, swore under his breath.

"Who the hell could sneak up on us like that?"

"That bloody chief and his cronies!" replied Jake.

He felt a deep rage boil in his chest. Whoever had taken her was going to regret it.

Lecky marched over to Dunmore, his voice tight with restrained fury.

"You fell asleep? On watch?"

Dunmore scrambled to his feet, eyes wide.

"I didn't mean to...I was just closing my eyes for a second..."

Jake stepped in, fists clenched at his sides.

"A second was all they needed! She's gone, and we've no idea how long ago!"

Lecky shouldered his rifle, his expression colder than usual.

"You had *one* job, Dunmore. Just *one*".

Dunmore looked down, shame written all over his face.

Lecky took a slow breath, forcing himself to focus.

"Alright...no point yelling now. We don't know where or how far they are, but we've got tracks, and we've got daylight, so let's get moving...fast".

"We should just leave her," Dunmore huffed, dabbing at his sweat-soaked forehead with a silk handkerchief, "it's a bloody jungle. She's probably dead already".

The words had barely left his mouth when Jake's fist crashed into his jaw with a sickening crack.

Dunmore staggered backward, slamming into a tree before sliding to the ground, blood trickling from his nose.

"You lunatic!" he shouted, "I think you broke my nose!"

Jake stood over him, flexing his fist. His voice was low and ice-cold.

"Say that again you bastard, and I'll knock your teeth so far down your throat you'll have to stick your toothbrush up your arse to clean them!"

Dunmore glared but stayed silent, the message clearly received.

Tariq stepped between them.

"Enough. We are wasting time...we must go after our friend...now!"

Everyone sprang into action. Shelters were quickly dismantled, equipment stuffed in packs, and weapons checked with urgent hands. Jake bungyed Evelyn's pack to his, and slung both uneasily over his shoulder. The footprints led east, deeper into the jungle, threading between roots and weaving through ferns already beginning to rise in the warming morning light.

Jake glanced at the trail.

"They didn't even try to hide their tracks".

Tariq nodded grimly.

"They did not need to. They think we will not catch them".

Lecky cast one last look at the remnants of Evelyn's abandoned shelter.

"Smart asses...time to prove them wrong".

Without another word, they set off at a trot, following the line of bare footprints into the green shadows - hearts pounding, weapons ready, and minds racing with every possibility; no one willing to say out loud what they feared most.

The jungle swallowed them almost immediately.

Vines snagged at their legs, branches whipped their faces, and the thick undergrowth clawed at every exposed inch of skin. A pair of jaguars watched them through the vegetation, saliva drooling from their mouths. But the team did not slow. The trail was clear - foot prints crushed into damp soil, a broken twig here, a displaced fern there.

The humidity was stifling; each breath feeling like a drag through a wet cloth, but Jake didn't slow. His pulse thumped in his ears as they rushed to close the gap. The trees towered above them like silent witnesses, and the path became increasingly difficult, with thick vines curling from the ground and massive roots snaking across the trail. But they didn't let up, the soft thud of their boots the only sound, aside from the occasional rustle in the bushes.

Lecky cursed as he tripped over a root, nearly face-planting into the mud, but he didn't stop. They all kept moving, driven by the same need. They had to catch up. They had to.

Jake ran near the front, eyes darting constantly, his rifle bouncing against his chest with every stride. He hadn't said a word since they left, straight faced, gaze fixed on the path ahead like it owed him answers, scanning for prints, looking for anything that would give them a clue - an extra scuff mark, a change in direction, anything.

"Evelyn's tough," Lecky panted from behind, "she'll be fine".

"She shouldn't *have* to be," Jake snapped, not slowing his pace.

Dunmore, the cause of their current predicament, lagged at the rear, whilst Mateo searched ahead for more tracks.

He called back, "Still fresh! Maybe thirty minutes ahead, no more!"

Tariq was already ahead of him, slipping between tree trunks like a shadow.

"Then we *can* catch them".

A sharp cry rang out - not human, some jungle bird startled by their pounding feet. Jake flinched but didn't stop. Sweat poured down his back. He could feel Evelyn's pack dragging at his shoulder, a constant reminder of what was at stake.

They hit a narrow ravine, and Jake didn't hesitate. He skidded down the bank, boots digging into loose earth, landing hard and rolling up in one smooth motion. Each man took their turn sliding down the slope. Lecky followed, less graceful, tumbling in a flurry of curses and mud.

Dunmore trailed at the rear, grumbling and gasping, but no one waited for him.

At the far side of the ravine, Mateo paused and pointed.

"There...see the scuff marks on that root? Someone stumbled".

"Not Evelyn," Jake said instantly, "too light-footed...one of them".

Tariq glanced back, pausing for a moment.

"They are carrying her".

Jake's stomach twisted. Was she unconscious? Was she injured? Or worse?

A low growl of thunder rumbled in the distance. Somewhere ahead, a monkey screamed. They pushed on, deeper and darker now. The canopy thickened overhead, filtering out the sun and draping everything in a greenish gloom. Time blurred into motion - mud, sweat, breath, heartbeat, repeating itself.

And then - Mateo threw up a hand.

"Wait!"

The group skidded to a halt, gasping, weapons raised.

Mateo crouched low again, fingers tracing something in the dirt.

"A drop of blood".

Jake's chest clenched.

"It could be one of *them*," Tariq offered, but even he didn't sound convinced.

Jake's voice was urgent.

"Faster...come on!"

Tariq's voice cut through the heavy air.

"Too much jungle...they will be using the terrain to confuse us I think".

Jake's gaze snapped to the dense foliage ahead. They weren't going to get an easy break. He knew it. They were going to have to push harder. The team was already drenched in sweat, faces strained, but there was no choice.

"Keep moving," Jake shouted, his voice tight with worry and frustration.

Lecky grinned through his exhaustion.

"Guess we'll be jungle experts by the time this is over".

"I'll settle for catching *them* first," Jake muttered, eyes locked on the path ahead.

Every nerve in his body was screaming to go faster, to catch them, and rescue Evelyn.

Then, suddenly, through the maze of leaves and branches, a flicker of movement. His heart stopped. A figure. Barely visible.

Jake raised his rifle, instincts kicking in, but it was gone before he could make a move. A shadow. An illusion. But it *had* been there.

"Did you see that?" Jake called out.

No one had.

Jake wiped his brow and took a sip from his canteen.

"I must be going mad," he thought to himself.

The trail took another sharp turn, following the edge of a steep hill. The jungle ahead seemed quieter, the usual chorus of birds and insects silenced by the thickening atmosphere. Jake's skin crawled. Something was off.

And then, a shout - distant, but unmistakable...Evelyn.

Jake's heart lurched. She was alive. But they were still too far away.

Adrenaline surged through his body as he pushed forward, faster now, faster than he thought he could go. He wasn't waiting. Not this time.

Tariq was already ahead, his dark silhouette a blur through the green. Mateo and Lecky followed close behind, and even Dunmore had found a second wind, though he still cursed loudly with every misstep.

As they moved - more hurried now - every sense screamed. Evelyn was close. They had all heard it, and Jake could feel it. Smell it in the air. The fight wasn't over. Not yet. And if these bastards thought they could just walk off into the trees with her, then they were about to learn just how wrong they were.

Evelyn's heart pounded in her chest, each beat a desperate reminder of her vulnerability. She twisted and pulled against the ropes binding her wrists and ankles, but the fibres bit into her skin, cutting deeper with each movement. Her fingers were stiff from the effort, her skin raw and red where the crude ropes dug into the delicate flesh. They had stripped her completely, leaving her exposed to the cool evening air, the flickering glow of the fire casting twisted shadows across her body.

Around her, the warriors circled like wolves, their eyes wide with a mixture of curiosity and something darker. Their murmurs rose in a low, grating chorus as they stared at her, whispering to one another in a language she didn't understand. She could feel their hands brushing her skin, tentative at first, as if testing the softness of her flesh. Their fingers caressed her arms and the bare expanse of her neck, tracing the lines of her blonde hair as if they had never seen anything so foreign before.

Her pale skin seemed to hold an otherworldly quality to them, her blonde hair shimmering in the firelight like strands of gold. They were fascinated by her, mesmerized, as if she were something that didn't belong - something they were desperate to understand.

The chief stepped forward then, his presence commanding attention. He approached her with deliberate slowness, his eyes taking in every detail of her body with a strange, almost clinical interest.

He reached out with one calloused hand, fingers rough and steady as he tilted her chin upward, forcing her to meet his gaze. His eyes studied her face, every inch of it, as if she were a relic uncovered from the earth after centuries of slumber. She could feel his breath, warm against her skin, as he examined her with a disquieting intensity, and then her worst fears began to take shape as he began to caress her naked breasts, running his tongue along one of them, whilst simultaneously the tribesmen wailed like animals, thrusting their hips backwards and forwards in anticipation. Evelyn was powerless, raising her eyes up at the jungle canopy in an attempt to block out what was happening, and what was *going* to happen.

But she refused to show fear. Her teeth were clenched tightly together, and her eyes flashed with defiance as she glared up at the chief.

"Is your *very* tiny willy getting excited?" she calmly uttered.

He did not understand but just laughed a gruesome laugh, his face now level with hers. At this Evelyn took her opportunity, she had nothing to lose after all, and head butted him viciously, catching him directly on the nose.

"Stitch that you bastard!" she shouted, "when I get out of this, I'm kicking you right in the..."

But before she could finish the sentence, the silence shattered. A loud bang split the air as the jungle exploded with the sharp cracks of gunfire, each shot sounding like thunder. The warriors froze, their eyes darted toward the strange sound, panic quickly replacing the strange fascination as they scattered in terror, their eyes wide with confusion and fear as bullets sliced through the dense foliage above their heads, some slamming into trees and leaving splintered trunks in their wake. The ground seemed to tremble under the force of the shots, and the warriors' weapons clattered to the dirt, forgotten in their panicked flight. Evelyn barely had time to react as chaos erupted around her. The chief jerked back, his hands instinctively reaching for a weapon. Evelyn's pulse surged, this was her chance. The firelight flickered erratically as the night air filled with the sharp echo of gunshots, the promise of salvation growing nearer with each passing moment.

Jake and the others burst into the clearing, their rifles raised, their eyes scanning the area for Evelyn. The sight of her, bound and exposed, hit him like a physical blow. She was tied to a wooden post, completely naked, her body raw from the ropes that had held her captive. For half a second, Jake froze, his breath catching in his throat as he fought back the surge of anger and concern. But then he snapped into action, shrugging off his jacket and quickly tossing it over her shoulders.

Tariq cut the ropes with a single motion, and Evelyn's arms fell free. Jake stepped forward, his voice trembling with concern.

"Are you alright?"

Evelyn smirked, despite herself, her voice calm even through the haze of fear and anger.

"I was fine until you lot started shooting and gave them a reason to kill me".

Jake grunted in reply, helping her to her feet and making sure she was covered. Around them, the chief and his warriors were on their knees, hands raised in surrender, their eyes bulging with terror. The sound of gunfire had done its job. These outsiders were not to be trifled with.

The chief mumbled something, his voice shaky, but Evelyn's gaze never wavered. She stepped forward, adjusting Jake's jacket around her shoulders as she met the chief's eyes. For a moment, there was an eerie silence. Then, without warning, she drew her leg back and slammed her foot squarely into the chief's groin. The sound of his agonised yelp rang out, and he doubled over, clutching himself in pain, his face a twisted mask of shock and agony.

Jake couldn't suppress a grin, shaking his head.

"You really specialise in that move, don't you?"

Evelyn shrugged, unbothered.

"It's always a crowd pleaser".

As the team gathered their gear, ready to leave, their eyes fell on the warriors still kneeling in fear. But there was something else - a disturbing sight. Several of the warriors were wearing pieces of Evelyn's clothing. Her shirt was draped over one of their shoulders, her boots on the feet of another, and her trousers were now worn by the chief himself. They had taken what they could, without hesitation, as if it were their rightful spoils. Her undergarments were nowhere to be seen, but it was clear from the warriors' dishevelled appearances that they had claimed her belongings, unbothered by how it had come to be theirs.

It was an unsettling image - her clothing, once her protection and dignity, now worn by the very people who had captured and humiliated her. The absence of any remorse from the warriors only made it more grotesque. They were like vultures, picking at the remnants of their prey without a second thought.

Evelyn's lips tightened as she surveyed the scene, her gaze cold. She motioned for each of the tribe to hand back her clothing, growling in Spanish at the chief to translate. One by one each man tossed their spoils to the ground. Her anger flared again, but this time, it was controlled, lethal. Without a word, she reached into her pack and pulled out her pistol, the cold steel a familiar weight in her hand. Her eyes never left the chief as he struggled to recover from the blow she had delivered to his groin. He was still shaking, his face pale with pain and fear, but he held his ground, defiant in his surrender.

She quickly raised her pistol. The sound of the shots reverberated around the clearing as the first bullet struck the chief squarely in the groin. His yelp was strangled, his body jerking forward, and he collapsed onto the dirt, gasping for breath. The second shot rang out, and his head snapped back as the bullet struck, his skull caving in with a sickening crack. He crumpled to the ground, his body twitching for a moment before falling still.

The remaining warriors, still too terrified to move, stared in shock as Evelyn calmly lowered her weapon. They had heard the deafening sounds of the gunfire, but this - this was something else. They had never seen death like this. It was clean and efficient. They had only ever known the slow, brutal violence of their own people's way of fighting.

Evelyn quickly turned to Jake, her left hand held out in anticipation.

"Your pistol".

Jake was caught off guard.

"What?"

"Give me your pistol...quick!" Evelyn retorted.

Jake pulled his pistol from its holster and placed it in Evelyn's open hand.

Without hesitation, Evelyn continued her work, moving with cold, calculated precision. She picked off the remaining warriors one by one, using both weapons, her shots clean and swift. The jungle, already alive with the sounds of the earlier chaos, fell silent once more as each warrior crumpled to the earth in a bloody heap, their bodies falling with terrifying speed, their blood staining the earth, mixing with the damp soil beneath them.

The rest of the team, eyes averted in grim respect for the carnage unfolding before them, were silent. Even Dunmore's leering grin faltered as he saw Evelyn's cold, methodical efficiency. He quickly looked away, but the image of her - calm, collected, and ruthless - was burned into his mind.

With the last of the tribe members dead, the clearing was eerily quiet, save for the faint rustle of leaves stirred by the wind. Evelyn stood amidst the bodies, her breath steady, her expression impassive, as though she had simply carried out a task. The two pistols gleamed in the low light, their barrels still smoking, whilst Jake's jacket hung loosely around her shoulders.

"Cheers Jake," she said as she calmly handed him his weapon.

She then wiped the blood from the barrel of her own gun with the sleeve of the jacket, and slid the pistol back into its holster as if it were nothing more than an everyday action.

Evelyn stood for a moment, almost admiring her work.

"That is for what you did, were about to do, and for all the women in the world who never get *real* justice".

Jake approached her, his face hardening as he looked at the aftermath.

"It's probably not a good question, but are you sure you're alright mate?"

Evelyn didn't flinch, didn't blink. Her voice was calm, almost indifferent.

"Better than I was, thankfully it was only their *eyes* that were pleasured," she replied, her voice distant, almost detached as she wiped the blood from her hands with a large fern leaf. Her eyes seemed unfocused, her mind far from the clearing now stained with the remnants of the warriors.

"I suppose that makes me a murderer now?"

Mateo, who had remained silent throughout the bloodshed, stepped closer. He placed a hand on her shoulder, his touch surprisingly gentle.

"No one even knew this tribe existed, so they will not be missed" he said, "and besides...they deserved it".

Evelyn didn't answer at first. She just stood there, staring at the bodies that now littered the clearing, the jungle around them strangely quiet. Then she snapped out of it.

"Yes, you're right...arseholes...anyway I'd better get some clothes on, it's getting a bit chilly and I don't want you boys getting a cheap thrill do I?"

Jake helped her gather up the clothes that the tribe had taken, then shielded her as she retrieved some underwear and clothing from her pack and got dressed. She stared at the now tainted clothing lying on the ground at her feet and turned to Jake.

"You know I'm not going to let this get to me. I'm lucky, they just ogled at my body; worse has happened to others. As for my clothes, I'll just wash the odour of these tossers from them in that pot of water over there and they'll be right as rain".

Jake nodded, and held out his arms.

"Give us a bloody hug".

Evelyn smiled and accepted the offer willingly, falling into Jake's arms, clinging to him tightly, and kissing him on the cheek.

"I love you, you know, and I'm never letting you go".

Jake laughed then stared into her eyes.

"Like peas in a pod eh? I love you too Evie," he said in a low voice, "now let's get out of here".

Before they departed, Evelyn knelt beside the chief's body and calmly searched him. She found the astrolabe and the black stone tucked inside a pouch - relics from a lost world. They weren't essential to the mission, but she couldn't leave them behind to rot in the dirt. Some things were too old, too powerful, to be forgotten.

Jake watched as Evelyn carefully stowed the items away in her pack, his gaze lingering on her. He had seen her kill before, but this...this was different. The violence had been swift, calculated, and ruthless, and Evelyn, cold as steel, had done it without hesitation.

No one spoke. The team moved like ghosts, even the clumsy Dunmore, in grim silence. The black stone pulsed faintly in Evelyn's pack, whilst the astrolabe, ancient and fragile, lay beside it.

"Let's get the flock out of here," Jake called out, his eyes flicking back toward the native camp.

Evelyn gave a short nod and turned without a word. The jungle closed around them, swallowing their trail as they vanished into the green.

CHAPTER 8

EVERY SHADOW A SUSPECT

The humidity in jungle was stifling and uncomfortable, as they trudged through the thick underbrush. The death of the tribesmen was still fresh in their minds, but no one spoke much - there was nothing left to say.

After about an hour of steady hiking, with the team moving closely in a single line formation, Evelyn heard it first: a sharp crack, distant but unmistakable.

A gunshot.

The sound carried through the jungle, its echo reverberating off the thick foliage, and for a moment, the world seemed to pause.

"Did you hear that?" Jake asked.

Evelyn's hand instinctively went to the grip of her pistol, its holster attached to a belt round her waist.

"I heard it," she said, eyes searching the shadows ahead, "I think it came from behind us".

Jake halted in his tracks.

"Well it can't be anyone from the tribe, they don't have guns".

Dunmore, who had been lagging a little behind, slowed his pace, his eyes darting nervously.

"What if it's those Templar fellows?"

"We can't afford to find out," Jake said, his voice calm but urgent, "stay alert and keep moving, and no more chopping at the jungle, just move gently, keep off the mud if you can, and try to leave no trail".

Evelyn felt her pulse quicken.

"I don't like this at all," she muttered, her voice quiet as she quickened her pace.

They continued onward, determined to remain as quiet and stealthy as possible, their eyes scanning the surroundings for any sign of movement as they tried not to disturb the foliage of the forest, slipping between tree trunks and ducking under vines, veering from their course every few hundred yards, zigzagging rather than walking a straight path. The inhospitable jungle forced them to adapt - skirting thickets, climbing over massive roots, wading through shallow marshes where needed. But no more sounds came from behind, instead they were serenaded by the shrieks of birds and screeching and clicking of insects.

It gave them no comfort.

Up ahead, the terrain dropped sharply. Jake held up a hand, halting the line.

They had come to a ravine - narrow, but deep, its moss-covered walls shiny and wet. A fast-moving stream roared far below, churning over sharp, uneven rocks. One missed step and it was a straight fall resulting in possible broken bones or worse.

"No way round it?" Lecky asked, already knowing the answer.

"Not without adding hours to the route," Jake replied, visually searching the far side.

There was a fallen tree bridging the ravine - a natural crossing, but barely wide enough for a foot. The bark was stripped, leaving it smooth and damp. One slip, and they would be gone.

Jake sucked in a breath.

"Okey dokey everyone...one at a time. Make sure your weapons and kit are secure first...and don't look down".

Tariq turned to Evelyn.

"Just like in the Crystal cave..."

Evelyn smiled as she remembered.

"Yes, but a little bit higher this time," she replied, "come on then Indiana let's get to it".

Dunmore scoured the terrain before piping up.

"I'll go first. I'm the steadiest".

Evelyn and Tariq glanced at each other in disbelief, whilst Jake pointed toward the tree bridge.

"Steadiest? You're always falling over yourself mate, but...be my guest".

Dunmore nodded and stepped up onto the log, arms out for balance. He moved slowly, deliberately, like a tightrope walker, every muscle tensed. Midway across, a bird burst from the brush nearby, and for a moment he wobbled - but righted himself. The others instinctively looked away, but moments later, he made it to the far side and proudly crouched down, waving them on.

"What the hell was that?" Jake exclaimed as he calmly sat down and straddled the log, slowly edging himself across, "no use killing yourself...this is how to do it".

One by one, the rest of the team followed. As Evelyn dragged herself across, her heart was pounding - not from fear of the height, but the ever present feeling of being watched. She paused halfway and glanced back into the jungle.

Nothing.

Still, the hair on her neck stood up.

Once across she stepped onto solid earth beside the others, allowing herself a single breath of relief. They were still alive.

But the silence behind them felt heavier than before. Too heavy.

Lecky was the last one across and before continuing on he and Jake stared over to where they had just come from. Something, or someone, was still out there, and they hadn't given up.

The team checked weapons and packs then moved on quickly, travelling in a tighter formation. The further they marched, the more the foliage began to thin; the trees sparser, the undergrowth giving way to moss covered stone and wind worn rock. The sounds changed too - less insect noise, more distant wind, and the occasional lonely birdcall.

By mid-afternoon, the jungle had given way entirely to rough foothills. Towering cliffs loomed ahead, sharp-edged and dry, rising like jagged teeth against the grey-blue sky. The ground crunched beneath their feet, a mix of gravel and dry soil. The temperature dropped as they ascended, the air becoming thinner, crisper, and somehow ancient, as if it hadn't been breathed in centuries.

Jake paused to admire the new terrain.

"Here, didn't that priest bloke say the city was in the jungle?"

Evelyn took off her hat for a moment and scratched her head.

"Perhaps it turns into jungle later on".

"At this altitude? You're having a laugh," Jake replied.

Their pace slowed. Every breath was harder won.

They followed a winding trail carved by water and time, moving along narrow valley floors where echoes followed them like ghosts. A mist rolled down from the peaks, curling low and cold around their ankles. And there, tucked against a boulder like forgotten history, were the bones.

Jake saw them first and raised a hand.

Half-buried in shards of scree, a skeleton lay sprawled on its back, ribs jutting through rotted leather. A rusted helmet still clung to the fractured skull, split cleanly down one side. A few feet away, another corpse had collapsed face-first, its corroded breastplate torn open as if cleaved by something impossibly strong. One skeletal hand stretched toward a broken sword, lying just out of reach, the blade cracked, dulled by centuries of rain and regret.

More bones appeared the further they looked - some torn apart and scattered like they had been thrown, others collapsed where they had fallen; curled into the final moments of a desperate retreat. Torn boots, snapped bones, rusted hilts - all strewn across the rock like relics of a forgotten massacre.

"Definitely Conquistadors," whispered Evelyn, crouching to inspect one of the corpses, touching the edge of a shattered cuirass, "they must have escaped the city...tried to make it out".

Jake stepped carefully around a collapsed ribcage, his eyes scanning the slope.

"They didn't get far then did they?" Jake replied.

"Not by the looks of it," replied Evelyn.

She stood slowly.

"Something hunted them down".

Mist thickened again, curling around the dead like a shroud, and for a long moment, no one spoke.

The jungle, as always, remained silent. Watching.

Dunmore gazed for a moment at the centuries old carnage then shuffled back, wiping a hand over his mouth.

"Well, this all very comforting".

"Not for these blokes though," said Jake to Dunmore, "it looks like *your* ancestor scarpered and left them to it".

A low growl interrupted him. It came from up the trail. The team froze.

A moment later, the jaguar stepped into view – as dark as a shadow, its muscles rippling under a black coat dappled in almost invisible black rosettes. Its eyes locked on them, unblinking.

Evelyn didn't move.

"Don't run," she whispered, "whatever you do, don't run".

Jake's hand moved slowly to his weapon. Lecky reached for the flare gun instead, the only thing with a chance of scaring it off without bringing the whole mountain down on them.

The jaguar padded forward, low and silent. Twenty feet. Fifteen. Ten.

Lecky fired.

A sudden burst of red light and smoke hissed through the air. The jaguar recoiled with a snarl, then leapt sideways into the undergrowth, vanishing as quick as it had appeared.

Silence again. But the kind charged with adrenaline.

Jake exhaled.

"Well I'm not hanging round here to see if he has any mates...come on..."

They moved quickly now, the mountain path rising steeply ahead, every shadow and overhang suddenly suspect. The jungle was far behind them, swallowed by the thick mist below. Here, the world had changed. Whatever waited ahead felt older, colder - carved into the stone long before men walked upright.

The trail twisted like a scar along the cliffside, narrowing with each step. Loose dirt and stones shifted treacherously underfoot, tumbling away into nothingness. Above, the peaks were lost in cloud, and the wind had sharpened into something cruel - thin and icy, slicing through their clothing and biting at any exposed skin.

The air grew thinner still, drier, each breath burned a little deeper in their lungs, and conversation faded to grunts and nods, replaced by the rasp of breath and the crunch and slide of boots on rock. Muscles ached with the climb, but no one stopped. The silence was immense - too immense.

By the time the sun dipped low behind the tall ridges, they had climbed well above the tree line. The vibrant jungle was no more than a green smear beneath a rolling tide of mist. Up here, there was only grey stone, constant wind, and the looming sense that they had stepped into a place the world had long forgotten.

Then it came into view.

Perched on a crag jutting out from the mountain like a broken tooth were the ruins - ancient, weathered, and strangely elegant against the bleak surroundings. Their approach had followed what must once have been a road - now barely more than a series of uneven flagstones choked with lichen and frost.

Chiselled into the face of the mountain was a massive stone archway, half-collapsed, flanked by towering statues worn faceless by time. Each figure had once held something in their hands, but only broken stumps remained. Moss clung to their feet like green flame.

Beyond the arch, walls of crumbling stone formed the outline of a forgotten settlement. Buildings with arched roofs sat in sunken plazas, their corners collapsed and their murals faded by centuries of wind and rain. Tall stone columns lay scattered like the bones of giants. A circular platform dominated the centre, edged with symbols that seemed to shift under the eye - half Incan, half something far older.

The most concerning of all was what they saw just ahead of the archway. Driven deep into the earth, stood a jagged iron spike, and upon it, rested a skull - weathered, sun-bleached, and unmistakably human. The tarnished rim of a conquistador's helmet still clung to the bone, the metal dented, twisted, as though struck by something brutal.

Lecky stopped in tracks some distance away and turned to Evelyn.

"Another one of your Spanish buddies I think..."

Jake stepped closer, his eyes fixed on the skull.

"I don't know about you lot but this seems like a bit of a warning to me".

No one disagreed.

Evelyn stepped forward slowly past the skull towards the village, her voice low and tinged with awe.

"I don't think this place was built by the people from the city we are searching for. This is older...much older".

Jake took in the surroundings.

"Looks like a good place to camp for the night though," he said, "high ground, good visibility *and* shelter".

"A home from home eh?" said Lecky, "vary rare in our line of work".

They moved in carefully, sweeping the area. An ancient tower, little more than a foundations and a low wall now, provided a vantage point. Inside one of the more intact structures - a square chamber with a domed ceiling - they found what remained of a fire pit and even the crumbling remnants of clay pots.

They set up camp there, lighting a small fire in the centre. The flames cast flickering shadows on the cracked stone walls, dancing over faded carvings - spirals, suns, serpents swallowing their own tails.

Outside, the wind howled through the broken columns.

The night was clear, and the mountain sky blazed with constellations they didn't recognise - alien shapes in the heavens. The temperature had plummeted, and their breath fogged in the air like ghosts.

Evelyn sat near the fire, the astrolabe in her lap, turning it slowly in her hands. The black stone sat nearby, wrapped in cloth. It pulsed faintly, as if responding to the altitude...or the ruins... or something beneath them.

"There's something buried here," she whispered, "I can feel it".

Jake didn't reply, but he nodded, his eyes fixed on the doorway, rifle across his knees.

"Do you believe it has power, like the Angel's Tear crystal we found in Afghanistan," asked Tariq.

Evelyn looked over to him.

"Maybe...I don't know...but I can definitely feel *something*".

In the stillness of that ancient ruin, surrounded by stone and silence, the team felt it too.

Lecky took the first watch at the tower, silhouetted against the stars, two-hour stags watching the valley below for any sign of pursuit. The cold had settled in with the darkness, creeping through layers of clothing and numbing fingers, noses, and toes. The wind howled intermittently down from the peaks, and each gust seemed to carry with it a whisper of something ancient.

The tower was perched high above the valley floor, on a narrow ledge just below the ridgeline. From this vantage point, they could see far across the undulating terrain - black silhouettes of crags and stone spires piercing the moonlit mist. Below, the jungle had vanished into a sea of cloud, and every now and then, the valley echoed with the far off cry of something unseen. Whether it was an animal or something else, none of them could tell.

Lecky had taken Dunmore to one side before sentry duty began.

"Don't screw this one up, Dunmore," he said, "you fall asleep again and I'll make sure you don't wake up next time".

Dunmore muttered something about being tired, but the look in Lecky's eyes silenced any protest.

And so, wrapped in ponchos and sleeping bags, rifles across their laps, they sat the long night in turns - each alone with their thoughts, watching the valley through tired, stinging eyes.

Lecky and Jake took the first two stags. Lecky was restless and didn't sit at all - he stood, hood up, rifle slung across his chest, eyes unblinking, barely moving, save to sweep the valley with his night vision binoculars. A soldier through and through.

Jake kept scanning the trail they had ascended, recalling the tense feeling in his chest when the jaguar had stalked them earlier that day. He couldn't shake the sense that something else was watching now - something worse.

Evelyn's turn was quiet. She sat still as a statue, the cold forgotten as her mind returned again and again to what she had done in the jungle. She clenched the astrolabe inside her pack without even realising it, as if afraid it might vanish or betray her somehow.

Mateo spoke silently in Spanish under his breath during his stag - old prayers, maybe, or curses aimed at the mountains, or fate itself.

When Dunmore's turn came, he huddled against the rock wall and forced his eyes wide open, repeating Lecky's warning in his head. He rubbed his arms furiously, cursing the wind and himself, shifting every few minutes to stop from drifting off. He thought of the riches and power he would soon possess, and this warmed his greedy heart.

The night passed in brittle silence. No sign of movement below. No sounds of a pursuit; and yet no one relaxed.

There was something in the wind - a warning, perhaps - and with dawn still hours away, the cold wasn't the only thing that made their breath catch in their throats.

Morning crept over the peaks in pale streaks of silver and grey, the sun still hidden behind the jagged spine of the mountains. The air remained bitingly cold, but the wind had eased, and for a few precious hours, there was no sound but the faint crackle of a small, controlled fire which they only lit again once daylight had arrived, for fear of it betraying their location.

Lecky knelt beside it, crouched low and flipping flat slices of bacon grill over a tiny stove built from three stacked rocks. The smell wasn't exactly pleasant - more like warmed-up dog food and old socks – but, added to the hot baked bins, dry crackers and tinned sausages, it was just right.

Jake sat propped up against the stone wall, steam rising from his mug of hot tea in his hands. Evelyn sat with her legs crossed, wrapped in her sleeping bag, staring out at the cloud-swathed valley below, whilst Mateo worked quietly nearby, slicing dried meat into strips and whispering prayers to himself.

Dunmore shuffled up, bleary-eyed, rubbing warmth back into his fingers.

"Well, well," Jake said with a smirk, not looking up, "the mighty Lord Dunmore stayed awake through his stag for once. Miracles *do* happen".

Evelyn didn't even try to hide her grin.

Dunmore groaned and dropped down beside them.

"Yes, well, Mister Leck here threatened to kill me if I nodded off again. Something about it being the *last* thing I ever did".

He looked across at Lecky, who didn't deny it – but just offered him a steaming mess tin of fried goodies, with a knowing smirk.

"*I* took it seriously," Dunmore said, accepting the tin with a shrug, "my life apparently depends on him not being in a bad mood".

"Smartest thing you've said all trip," Lecky replied, finally sitting down with his own meal.

Tariq was still on stag a few feet away, mess tin of food in his hand whilst he watched the valley below. They ate in silence for a moment, breaths steaming in the dawn light, the heat from the fire a small but welcome luxury.

Then Evelyn broke the quiet.

"So," she said slowly, warming her hands around her tea, "what exactly are we going to *do* with the 'Book of Truth' when we get home? Assuming we get out of this of course".

Jake exhaled through his nose, his gaze distant.

"That's the million dollar question, isn't it?"

"As long as we possess it, I think we'll be at risk forever," Evelyn said, "and not just from the Templars".

Lecky scoffed.

"We already are".

"That may be the case but I'm not talking about hit men or zealots," she said, "I'm talking about governments, institutions, the church and other religions. They'll bury us before they let it get out".

"But *should* it get out?" Tariq asked, more to the air than anyone. "Do we really want to hand over something *that* powerful to the world? What if it causes more chaos than clarity?"

"*I* think we should," replied Jake, "we *saw* the Garden of Eden...we *met* Jesus for heaven's sake...it's the right thing to do...and it's what *He* wanted".

"The word of the Lord eh?" added Lecky.

That hung in the air for a while.

Then Dunmore stabbed his fork into his sausages.

"Right. But we're also here for the gold, and the machine, remember? I say we let the world fight over the book and we retire rich and drunk on a beach somewhere".

Lecky gave him a flat look.

"We're here because some monk, priest, or whatever, sent you on a wild goose chase with half a map and a journal of half truths. If there *is* gold, it's not just lying around, and the machine will be protected - probably for a reason".

Dunmore smirked.

"Yes, but is that not the fun part?"

Jake gave a dry laugh.

"Fun's not the word I'd use".

Evelyn stood, brushing crumbs from her lap.

"Whatever's up there - gold, truth, or some ancient alien conspiracy - we'll find out soon enough. Let's just enjoy our breakfast in peace".

The fire hissed in reply, the smoke curling thin and grey into the morning air.

Mist coiled around the ruined archways like smoke from a long-dead fire. Now fed, the team stirred slowly, their muscles stiff from the climb and the cold, their nerves still raw from the jungle far below.

Evelyn had barely slept, having spent most of night turning the astrolabe in her hands until the first light crept across the mountain. Now, standing at the centre of the ruined plaza, she held it up again. The bronze dials shifted with a click. A beam of sunlight hit the face at an angle - and a faint glow pulsed from the carvings on the ground.

"Here," she said.

Jake joined her.

"Here?"

She nodded.

"I think there really *is* something beneath us".

Jake beckoned the others to join them and together they began clearing the moss-covered stone with careful hands. Beneath the vines and grit, they uncovered a circular slab carved with an intricate sun motif - golden rays stretching out from a central hole barely wide enough for a hand.

Jake tried to pry at it with his blade. The stone didn't budge.

Evelyn stepped forward again, holding the black stone now. As she brought it close, the centre of the disk shimmered, then slowly rotated. There was a low, grinding sound - ancient gears awakening after centuries - and the slab cracked down the middle, the doors swinging downwards revealing a narrow staircase, descending into blackness.

"Well I'll be..." whispered Lecky, peering in.

Jake flicked on his torch.

"Might as well take a look, while we're here. Grab your rifles though...just in case".

They descended in single file, weapons at the ready. The air grew colder with each step, thick with dust and the bitter tang of minerals. The walls of the tunnel were carved with brightly coloured scenes, preserved in the darkness - warriors in feathered helmets, a black sun, serpents with too many eyes. Some figures appeared to be kneeling in reverence before a floating stone shaped exactly like the one now in Evelyn's pack.

After a few minutes of descent, the tunnel opened into a vast subterranean chamber.

It took their breath away.

The room was impossibly wide, its ceiling lost in shadow, held aloft by massive pillars etched with unfamiliar symbols. The walls were adorned with ancient torches which Jake and Lecky lit with their lighters. The additional light revealed much. At the centre stood a dais of obsidian, surrounded by broken relics - bronze shields, shattered spears, and bones. Lots of bones. Some were human. Some... weren't.

Among them lay the twisted remains of what looked like Conquistadors - rusted armour, snapped swords, shattered muskets; helmets still bearing the cross of Castile. Skeletons slumped against walls, some reaching toward the exit as if clawing for freedom. One had died clutching a worn leather book, still bound by a rusted chain.

Jake crouched beside it, gently prying it free. The pages were brittle but intact, ink faded but legible. Spanish script filled every line, and sketches filled the margins - maps, symbols, and a familiar orb: the black stone.

"They found this place," Jake said, "and it killed them".

"But surely this isn't the lost city we are looking for?" said Evelyn, not expecting a reply.

On the dais lay a second black stone, slightly smaller than Evelyn's but engraved with similar glyphs. As she stepped forward, her own stone began to vibrate faintly in response.

A sudden, unexplained wind started to blow through the tunnels and a sound like whispering filled the chamber, coming from nowhere and everywhere. The torches flickered, and for the briefest moment, Evelyn thought she saw movement in the shadows - long, thin figures clinging to the walls, watching.

"Time to leave," said Dunmore, his voice quivering.

But none of them moved.

The black stone on the dais began to glow.

Evelyn stepped up onto the dais, the hum from her black stone rising in pitch as she approached the second one. The air felt charged now, like the moment before lightning strikes. Her outstretched hand hovered above the second stone. It pulsed, a heartbeat of light in the gloom.

"Don't touch it," Jake warned.

But she already had.

The moment her fingers brushed the surface, the chamber roared to life.

The whispering stopped - cut off in a single, suffocating instant. Then the humming deepened, lower and louder, until it was all they could hear, rattling in their bones. The light from both stones surged, merging in a flash that temporarily blinded them.

A shudder ran through the floor. Stone grated against stone. From the far wall, massive slabs began to shift, ancient mechanisms groaning as a part of the chamber opened like the jaws of a voracious animal. Beyond it: darkness, deeper than anything they'd seen yet. And in that darkness, something moved.

Not quickly. Not yet. But it moved.

The shadows stirred like smoke with weight, sliding down the wall, pooling along the floor. Eyes opened - far too many, glinting like wet obsidian; volcanic glass. Then the sound returned.

Not whispering.

Breathing.

Evelyn staggered back with the second stone in hand. It was hot now, searing through her glove. She stuffed it into her pack as Jake shouted, "GO!"

They turned and frantically ran for the stairs, boots hammering on the stone, the opening to the world now in sight. Behind them, something slithered with impossible speed, scraping across the floor and pillars. It hissed - not like a snake, but like air being sucked through teeth. As they reached the stairwell, Lecky turned to fire a burst into the dark, muzzle flashes strobing the cavern.

Nothing screamed, but the breathing paused.

Then it charged, hitting the base of the stairs just as Lecky launched himself upward, stone cracking and dust blasting through the tunnel. Something massive collided with the entrance, and for a few horrifying seconds the team thought it might squeeze through.

But it didn't.

The opening began to groan again – trying to close on its own as if it knew the terrors that were trying to escape.

Jake looked to Evelyn.

"The stones...quick!"

She yanked both from her pack and did the only thing she could think of, quickly slamming them together. The symbols aligned - click.

The stairwell shook. The ground trembled. Then... silence.

The opening sealed itself in a thunderclap of stone and dust.

They stood panting in the fresh air, hearts pounding. Somewhere below, the breathing faded...but didn't stop.

"Let's never do that again," muttered Jake.

Evelyn nodded, but her mind was already spinning. That thing...had been *guarding* something.

And now she had *both* stones.

CHAPTER 9

STRENGTH IN NUMBERS

In the cold morning light, the mountains seemed still, like they were holding their breath. The team stood at the threshold of the ruin, staring out across the windswept valleys below. The mountain air hit them like a wall - thin, cold, and sharp, scraping their lungs. The valley stretched far below, wide and open, ringed by snow-dusted ridgelines and uneven peaks that clawed at the sky. Behind them, the settlement's entrance was disguised within a sheer rock face - no sign of the horror they'd just escaped.

Lecky inhaled deeply, wiping dust from his face.

"I can breathe again, but it feels like knives".

Jake glanced over the edge, scanning the winding path that led down through the mountain pass.

"No jungle. No cover. If someone *is* following us..."

He didn't finish.

A sharp whistle echoed through the pass.

Evelyn's hand shot to her pistol.

Voices.

Figures moved up the trail toward them - six of them, armed but relaxed. And leading the way, grinning as if on a leisurely hike, was a broad-shouldered man with a crooked nose and the same arrogant swagger as Dunmore.

"Well, well, well!" the man called. "Would you look at that - baby brother, and still breathing".

Dunmore groaned.

"Oh, bloody perfect".

The man climbed the last few feet and spread his arms wide, as if expecting applause.

"Don't look so sour, Alex. You should be thrilled. Family reunion!"

"Everyone, meet my charming older brother," Dunmore muttered, "Richard".

Richard Dunmore tipped an imaginary hat.

"At your service. We've been following your little jaunt for a while now. Thought I'd let you do all the hard work".

His men fanned out, relaxed but watchful. They were all lean, weathered, and armed to the teeth - clearly professionals. Richard nodded toward Evelyn and Jake.

"I assume you've found something. Or else you wouldn't look quite so knackered. I've no interest in the drama - just the share I'm owed. You *are* looking for treasure, are you not?"

Evelyn folded her arms and glanced towards Lord Dunmore.

"Alex...who *is* this again?"

Dunmore cleared his throat.

"This is Richard...my older brother...and he is a bastard...my father apparently dabbled with one of the maids".

Jake nodded towards Richard.

"So, surely that makes you the *real* Lord if you are the oldest".

"It does. But I have no proof," Richard replied as he looked towards Dunmore, "and this *arse* won't take a DNA test".

"Perhaps we should just shoot him and take a sample," said Jake.

Richard looked over to his brother.

"Now that *is* a good idea".

Lecky laughed.

"Don't you just love these aristocratic family squabbles?"

"Well, squabble or not, you don't get a share just for showing up," said Evelyn.

Richard grinned.

"That's the thing about shares - they're negotiable. Especially when you've got information like, for instance, the other group I saw a day behind you. Ten men, dressed in black, armed, moving quickly".

Jake frowned.

"Templars?"

"Sorry old chap, I didn't get close enough to ask for identification, but I'd wager a few relics on it. They had the look. I've seen their sort before".

Evelyn exchanged a glance with Jake, then turned back to Richard.

"And you're not working with them?"

Richard laughed.

"Them? Their sort shoot first, lecture later. I'm far more agreeable. All I want is to walk out of this with a handful of history and both testicles intact. You've got two shiny stones and, I'm guessing, a rough idea of where the rest of this trail leads".

Jake narrowed his eyes.

"How much do you know?"

"Enough to know you're not out of the woods - or the mountains - yet. That old journal you have," Richard nodded toward Evelyn's pack, "might have the next piece of the puzzle. I'll offer a deal: you let me tag along, I help carry the load, keep an eye out for those zealots, and when we find the big score...I get my share. Or I take my chances and follow behind. Your call".

"Hold your horses there," said Lecky, as he looked over to Dunmore, "our share seems to be getting smaller by the day. How about you have some of *his* fifty percent?"

"That's fine by me...what do you say brother?" replied Richard.

Dunmore scowled.

"We should leave him here".

"But you won't," Richard smirked, "because I'm better company than the alternative".

The four friends huddled together for a moment then stood facing Dunmore and his brother.

Evelyn sighed.

"You can tag along, but all you get is part of *his* share, not ours".

Jake nodded.

"A few more guns are always welcome, but if you slow us down, you're gone".

Richard tapped two fingers to his brow.

"Scout's honour".

Jake and Lecky exchanged glances, then both looked over toward the five mercenaries he had brought along. Jake smiled and nudged Lecky with his elbow, then whistled to attract the attention of Evelyn and Tariq, gesturing with a nod towards the group of men.

"You seeing what I'm seeing?" he murmured.

Lecky squinted.

"Well I'll be a dirty name...Mackie and Parks".

"Oy...Mackie you scouse git!" Jake shouted.

"Flamin' Nora!" exclaimed Mackie as he recognised his friends, "small world eh?"

Without hesitation, the four strode over.

"You two lost?" Lecky called out with a grin.

Parks blinked in surprise, then laughed.

"Hey guys...Miss Kane...I sure didn't think we'd see you all again," he said, tipping his hat politely to acknowledge Evelyn.

Tariq offered his hand to both men.

"Hello my friends. How have you been?"

Parks shrugged.

"Left the army not long after you guys. Been doing private work - security contracts, extractions, escort jobs. Bit of a mixed bag. Not all of it legal, but it pays".

Jake gave a knowing nod.

"Yeah, we've been doing much the same. What's *he* paying you?"

"Not enough," Mackie said, "he called it a 'historical recovery mission.' Promised a generous chunk if it turned out to be worth anything".

Jake exchanged a glance with Lecky.

"Well, he's not wrong. The word is there's gold...perhaps a whole lost city's worth".

Mackie gave a low whistle.

"Wow that's smashin'. I always said you'd stumble across El Dorado one day".

Jake smirked.

"I've told your boss that all you get is part of *his* share, not ours".

Mackie raised his hands.

"Fair enough, mate. We're not greedy".

Jake quickly glance over his shoulder towards the two brothers.

"So, what do you think about your boss then?"

"He's a slimy tosser like most toffs," replied Mackie, "I wouldn't trust him as far as I could throw him".

Lecky grasped his shoulder.

"That's good to know bud".

"Well, it's good to have you on board. A few more guns are always welcome," Jake added.

The group set off down the pass, more watchful than ever. Evelyn pulled the book from her pack and opened it, flipping past diagrams and faded maps until she found a page with two matching symbols: the black stones. Below them, inked in spidery script, were some sort of coordinates - half rubbed away - and the name of a mountain no one had ever heard of.

She traced the letters with her finger.

"Monte Sangris".

Jake leaned in.

"Is that on any map?"

Evelyn shook her head.

"Not any modern one...well, I don't think so anyway".

"Well," Lecky said, scratching his head, "looks like we're heading for the mountain no one's ever heard of".

Jake looked thought back to the remains scattered along the trail.

"Let's hope we don't end up like those Spaniards".

"Amen to that," replied Lecky.

They walked for another hour, the trail narrowing until it was little more than a goat track clinging to the mountainside. The wind had teeth now, and even the toughened mercenaries in Richard's crew started glancing warily at the drop to their left.

Eventually, they rounded a bend - and stopped.

Before them stretched a rope bridge, sagging between two cliffs like the forgotten thread of some ancient spider. The bridge itself was a swaying tangle of ropes and timber, strung between two carved stone posts that rose from the rock like sentinels. It was long, narrow, and criminally thin, with slats of rotting timber spaced unevenly and ropes that groaned ominously in the breeze. The wooden slats looked ancient - blackened, cracked, and uneven - many missing altogether. Moss and fraying vines clung to the ropes, some strands visibly snapped.

It spanned a yawning chasm, easily a hundred metres deep and just as wide. The bottom was obscured by mist, but the distant roar of rushing water hinted at a river far below.

"Oh, fantastic," said Jake, "first a tree-bridge in the jungle, now this charming little death trap".

Richard leaned over to peer into the mist-shrouded abyss below.

"Well, at least it's consistent. You lot really know how to pick a scenic route".

"Is it even passable?" Evelyn asked, stepping carefully toward the edge.

Mateo nodded from the rear.

"Barely. These old ones were built by the Quechua...er...the Incas. Some are hundreds of years old. They knew what they were doing - but that does not mean it will not collapse under our weight".

"So...one by one again," said Lecky, already checking that his equipment was secure.

Dunmore looked at his brother.

"You first, since you're so keen on being part of the team".

Richard raised an eyebrow.

"You'd love that wouldn't you? Me tumbling to my death...but ladies first, brother. Manners, remember?"

"No...I don't mind if one of you goes first, honestly," said Evelyn.

"Let's just get this over with," Jake growled as he stepped forward, "I'll go first. If it holds me, it'll hold the rest of you. Unless Alex has been sneaking seconds again".

"Ha ha," Dunmore muttered, eyeing the rope uneasily.

The bridge swayed with every step Jake took, boards creaking like old floorboards in a haunted house. Halfway across, a gust of wind slammed into him, and he grabbed the side ropes hard. Boards shifted underfoot, and more than once, his boot slipped through a gap. But he didn't stop.

Behind him, Richard called out, "If you fall, try to scream something noble. We'll want a good story to tell".

Jake didn't answer, but just pushed on, keeping his eyes forward, breathing slow, until finally, he reached the other side.

One by one, the others followed. Evelyn went first, moving quickly, nimble and light, though her knuckles were white on the ropes. At the halfway mark, a gust of wind howled through the gorge, and the bridge lurched sideways. She dropped to one knee, heart hammering, then forced herself upright and continued on.

Tariq and Mateo were next with Dunmore closely behind. He cursed the whole way, swaying wildly with every step.

"If I die here, Lecky, I swear I'm haunting you," he shouted back.

"I'll take my chances," came the dry reply.

Lastly came Richard and his crew, with Richard calm and confident, even pausing to test a few knots and vines as he passed.

Lecky brought up the rear, keeping his eyes on everyone ahead and his hand close to his sidearm, just in case, whilst carefully stepping over a gap where a slat had completely vanished. Halfway across, he paused, glancing behind them.

The mountain was still. Silent. Watching.

Once they were all safely across, they stood together in the chill breeze, catching their breath. Lecky turned to look back at the bridge, now swaying gently behind them.

"That thing's held up for centuries," he said, "and it still scares the hell out of me".

"Everything up here's older than it should be," Jake replied, "and more dangerous than it looks".

"Well," said Evelyn, brushing her hair back from her face, "if that doesn't weed out the faint-hearted, nothing will".

Richard clapped his hands.

"Excellent. Now where's the next hazard? Pit trap? Rolling boulders? Rabid monks?"

"Just keep walking," Lecky said, "the sooner we're off this mountain, the better".

As they set off again, the mist began to lift slightly, revealing glimpses of stone ridges and narrow passes ahead - and somewhere beyond it all, the lost city where gold and power were waiting.

Ahead, the trail climbed once more, the wind carrying a strange, earthy scent on its breath - rich, floral, and unfamiliar. The canopy above thickened again, green against the grey, as if the mountain itself was hiding something high and impossible.

"I think we are close," Mateo whispered, almost reverently. "Very close".

The trail narrowed again, winding through a stand of crooked stone pillars that jutted from the earth like broken teeth. The air had grown still, the wind no longer howling but whispering - through cracks, over ridges, under breath.

Lecky slowed and glanced back the way they'd come.

"What is it?" Jake asked in a whisper.

"Thought I heard something. A scrape. Maybe a footstep".

Richard's team instinctively shifted, hands hovering near weapons. No one spoke. Even the birds had gone silent. A few stray rocks clattered down the cliff behind them - far too many for the natural wind.

Dunmore turned to Evelyn.

"It *could* be animals," he said, hopefully.

"Could be," she said, not sounding convinced, "but if it *is* the Templars..."

"They're good at this," muttered Richard, "ghosts in boots. They'll shadow you for days without a single glimpse, then strike when you least expect it".

"Comforting," Dunmore muttered.

"How do *you* know?" asked Evelyn, feeling a little suspicious at his knowledge of their pursuers.

Richard simply smiled and winked.

"Well they weren't that good in London *or* Puerto Maldonado," Jake reminded them.

They moved on, faster now, boots grinding on gravel and loose stone. But the feeling didn't go away - that prickling at the back of the neck, that sense of being watched just out of sight.

Every so often, someone would glance over a shoulder. Pause. Listen.

Nothing.

Still, they all felt it.

Richard's men tightened their formation slightly, Mackie their apparent leader, spreading just enough to cover each other's flanks.

At one point, Jake stopped dead, holding up a hand. The group froze.

Everyone strained their ears.

And there it was - faint, far back down the trail. A soft *clink*. Metal on rock.

Then nothing.

No voice. No movement. Just the heavy stillness of altitude and stone.

Jake spoke quietly.

"They're there. Watching. Waiting".

"Should we turn and face them?" asked Lecky.

Jake shook his head.

"Not yet mate. They haven't committed. If they're waiting for something, let's not give it to them".

Richard nodded grimly.

"I'd rather die in front of a treasure vault than on a dirt path halfway up a mountain anyway".

Jake looked to Evelyn.

"Anything in that book about this part of the trail?"

Evelyn shook her head.

"Nothing but warnings".

Of course there were.

The group pressed on, warier than before, every echo behind them now a question mark. And as the shadows grew longer across the rocks, each step forward felt like it was drawing them deeper into a web they couldn't yet see - but that was surely closing in.

Despite the tension, there was a subtle shift among the team - Jake and Lecky walking more easily now, the weight of suspicion somewhat eased.

Richard's men moved with the confidence of seasoned operators. Their eyes constantly scanned the ridgelines and the trail ahead, communicating with minimal words. They were ex-special forces - silent, deadly, and loyal to the job. Knowing some of them personally made the job a little easier for Jake and Lecky.

"If Richard tries anything clever," Jake muttered quietly to Evelyn, "his men won't back him. They're professionals. And they've got more loyalty to the mission - and to us - than to whatever fantasy or future plans old Dicky is chasing".

Evelyn gave a slight nod, keeping her eyes on the trail.

They made camp in a narrow alcove tucked into the cliffside, sheltered from the wind but offering little comfort. The fire was small again - just enough to boil water, cook, and warm hands. No one wanted light giving away their position. Above them, the stars blinked cold and distant. Below, the valley stretched into darkness, thick with mist and mystery.

Lecky took first watch, perched on a rock just outside the fire's reach, rifle butt resting against his shoulder. His silhouette was outlined in silver moonlight, motionless except for the occasional scan of the trail behind them.

Dunmore sat by the fire.

"Still awake," he muttered, glancing at Lecky with a smirk.

Jake grinned and passed him a dented canteen.

"Impressive".

"Fear does wonders for insomnia," Dunmore replied.

"Fair enough," Lecky called back without turning, "my threats are usually *very* motivating".

Evelyn sat down with the holy man's journal open on her lap.

"This whole trail was meant to disorientate," she said, "to separate, break trust, turn suspicion inward. That's what the warnings are really about".

There was a pause. The only sound was the wind brushing against rock.

Jake passed around metal cups.

"Not exactly the bedtime story I was hoping for".

Evelyn exhaled slowly, then Tariq spoke, his gaze fixed on the fire.

"I worry about the people who are following us, even more than the Taliban in Afghanistan. We still have our copies of the Book of Truth, and with us gone, the books are lost forever. The truth dies with us".

"Until some other silly sod finds the garden again," said Jake.

Evelyn nodded.

"And what about the city, and whatever's powering it?"

"Don't forget the gold," added Jake.

Dunmore stabbed at his beans with his spoon.

"And yet we keep going".

"Because we're all greedy bastards," Lecky called from his perch, "some of us for gold, some for glory, some for answers".

They sat in silence for a while, the fire crackling low. The warmth didn't reach far. Shadows clung to the walls. Even the stars seemed distant.

Somewhere far down the trail, a stone tumbled - just one - the sound carrying all the way up to them.

Everyone froze.

No movement. No voices. No second sound.

Just that one rock. As if something...or someone...had miss-stepped.

Jake stood slowly, hand on his pistol.

"No more stags alone tonight".

They nodded in agreement. None of them slept easily that night - not with the fire burning low, the stars overhead, and the certainty that something was coming.

Something close.

CHAPTER 10

AN UNWANTED PRESENCE

The narrow trail twisted between jagged outcrops and wind-carved stone. Somewhere below them the Templars moved in silence - ten figures, grey and black shadows flowing with eerie precision, their faces streaked with camouflage cream, boots soundless on the frozen path.

At their head walked Father Benedict, tall and skeletal beneath layers of wool and Kevlar, a silver crucifix gleaming at his chest. His skin was pale, untouched by sun or kindness. Eyes the colour of storm clouds scanned the mountainside with quiet determination.

Imam Qasim kept pace beside him, wrapped in a long coat, a carved ash staff in hand. His presence was calm but coiled - a scholar's posture, a soldier's readiness.

Behind them, Brother John paused with a thermal scope.

"They're camped near the lower ruins," he said, "I can see at least ten...maybe more. Looks like Dunmore's brother".

Benedict's mouth thinned.

"Then it *is* them?"

John gave a curt nod.

"It's them".

A gust of wind stirred the frost from the rocks. No one spoke.

Benedict came to a stop near a half-toppled monolith, brushing snow from its surface with a gloved hand. The stone bore faded markings - older than scripture, older than memory.

"They should not have come this far," he murmured, "none of them".

Qasim shifted his staff.

"Our masters will not tolerate their survival".

"No," Benedict said, "it must end here".

Brother John stepped over a fallen branch, scanning the ridge.

"We must move soon, before they vanish again".

Benedict raised a hand.

"No. Let them settle. Let the cold sap their strength. We'll strike when it hurts".

A sharp whistle signalled the halt. The men fanned out, settling beneath a natural overhang of broken rock and frost covered stone. No fires. No chatter.

They crouched low, wrapping themselves in sleeping bags, rifles across laps, blades checked in silence. Shadows swallowed them as the last light died behind the peaks.

Qasim unfurled a small prayer mat, kneeling without a word, whilst Benedict stood at the edge of the ledge, watching the darkness.

"They think the mountain will protect them," he said, "but it won't".

John adjusted his scope, settling against the rock.

"Dawn?"

Benedict nodded once.

"Dawn."

Qasim finished his prayer and rose, brushing frost from his sleeves.

"And if they run?"

"They will not get far," Benedict replied, "no one gets out".

Above, the stars pierced through drifting mist. Cold air settled like a shroud across the valley.

And the Templars waited - still as statues, their purpose carved into the frosty ground.

The stars were still out when Jake nudged Lecky awake with the toe of his boot. A light dusting of snow had fallen during the night transforming the scenery into a picturesque Christmas card.

"Come on, wakey, wakey," he whispered, "time to go".

Lecky groaned, pulling himself upright.

"I was dreaming of bacon. *Real* bacon. None of that dried cardboard crap in those tins".

"Tragic. We'll hold a memorial for your breakfast later".

Camp broke in minutes. No fire, no chatter, each of them quickly consuming whatever cold food they had to hand. Tariq scouted ahead with Mackie and Parks, while Evelyn quietly doused the last embers of the fire, her breath rising in ghostly wisps.

Richard tightened his boots.

"Why are we leaving before dawn, exactly?"

Jake gave him a pointed look.

"Because I like being alive. That reason work for you?"

Lecky smirked, slinging his pack on.

"Besides, you snore loud enough to give away our position anyway. Better we keep moving before they follow your symphony".

"*I do not snore,*" Richard muttered.

They slipped out just after four, descending into a narrow cleft between the rocks. Snow glittered underfoot. Tariq, joined by Mateo, led them through an ancient track hidden between fallen boulders – steep and awkward.

"Hopefully this snow will melt soon so they can't just follow our footprints," said Jake.

Everyone was vigilant, watching the ridgeline, and constantly glancing behind them. Nothing moved. But they all felt it - the pressure building like a storm on the horizon.

"Don't suppose we could ask them nicely to piss off?" Mackie whispered.

"Templars? They're more likely to ask *us* to lie down and bleed quietly" Jake replied.

"Charming people," said Mackie.

Jake laughed to himself recalling an old Monty Python sketch.

"No one expects the Spanish Inquisition".

Mid-morning, high above the ruins, the Templars arrived at the now empty camp, having been delayed due to their own misjudgement of the terrain.

Smoke still curled weakly from blackened stones. A few footprints, half-melted by the sun, circled the old wall from where they had kept watch.

"They left early," Brother John said, crouching by the remnants of the fire, "long before sunrise. They are many hours ahead now".

"They are getting smarter," Qasim noted.

"No," Benedict said, scanning the distant peaks, "they have *always* been smart".

He gestured, and the group spread out, moving as silent as falling ash. Although the snow had turned to slush John could still make out faint imprints of many feet.

"This way," he said, pointing upwards.

Benedict gave a short nod.

"Then we follow...and this time, we do not lose them".

Without another word, they melted into the stone and shadow, chasing ghosts along a mountain trail.

The landscape began to shift again as they pressed on, climbing steadily higher into the range. The bare stone and scree beneath their boots gave way to smoother plateaus of pale rock, the wind cutting cold and thin around them. Here and there, snow still clung to the shadowed cracks. Breathing was harder now, every step heavier than the last, and the sun above seemed smaller, paler, like it too struggled to reach this forgotten place.

Then everything seemed to change.

It began with a strange warmth rising from the stone underfoot. The air softened, becoming thick and damp. Jake slowed, taking in the changing surroundings. The others followed suit as moss began to appear, clinging to cracks in the rocks; and then, impossibly, they rounded a ridge and saw it.

A valley stretched below them, walled in on all sides by razor sharp peaks - but instead of snow and ice, it boiled with life.

A rainforest.

Lush and green and steaming, its canopy rippled with unseen movement. Tendrils of mist curled skyward like smoke, and brilliant birds scattered into the air in startled bursts of colour. It was utterly silent except for the low, ever present sounds of the jungle breathing. Everyone looked on with awe and surprise.

The trail narrowed to a switchback, much like the winding roads with 180 degree hairpin bends you would expect to see in places like Monaco, and they descended, drawn by the impossible. The jungle accepted them without a sound, closing in around the path. The heat was immediate - damp, pressing, and almost sweet smelling. Leaves broader than shields arched overhead, and roots as thick as tree trunks crawled across the path like sleeping serpents. Somewhere in the distance, something large gave a coughing growl.

Hours passed. Or maybe only moments. It was hard to tell anymore. Then they saw it.

At first it was just shapes in the shadows. Columns, maybe. Stone terraces. Then domes emerged from the jungle floor, choked in vines but whole. Great plinths etched with worn glyphs. A causeway, still intact, leading straight ahead into the undergrowth. Then an archway - moss-draped, majestic - looming above them like the mouth of some ancient god.

They had found it.

The lost city.

Evelyn took a cautious step forward, her heart thundering. It was real. Every wild theory, every scrap of research, every sleepless night and step taken in the Andes - it had all led to this.

She looked back at the others.

Even Dunmore's brother had gone silent.

But it didn't feel abandoned. The city was not a ruin. It was as fresh as the day it had been constructed.

Ash clung to a nearby stone, fresh, undisturbed.

And near a stairway, Evelyn spotted it - a footprint. Bare. Human. Recent.

One of the first things they all noticed was the light. Not sunlight, but a strange silver glow that filtered down through the impossibly lush canopy, casting dappled patterns on stone buildings that shouldn't have existed. Towering ziggurats, bridges of living vines, aqueducts still flowing with crystal clear water - all of it perfectly intact; untouched by time or the decay of the jungle surrounding it.

Lecky stood with his mouth open.

"This shouldn't be here. Not at this altitude. Not in this condition".

"It's like the jungle's growing *around* it, not over it," Evelyn said, brushing her fingers along a smooth column carved with ancient symbols.

"It's like it's...alive," Jake said, his voice hushed.

And then they saw the figures.

At first, they were shadows - watchers. Flickers of movement between the leaves. Silent, poised. Human in shape but clad in ceremonial hides and bright feathers, bodies painted with glowing pigments. The ancient tribe still lived here. Somehow, they had survived – hidden from the modern world; protected - and they were not alone.

Emerging from the city's deeper corridors were others - taller than any human, lithe and symmetrical, with skin the colour of polished obsidian and eyes like pools of mercury. These beings did not speak, but when one stepped forward, the air around them shimmered.

The sound came *not* through ears but through thought, a voice inside each person's mind - calm, curious, utterly alien.

"*I am called Ralos,*" the being said, "*you have come far. You seek the lost, but it was never lost*".

The team froze, instinctively reaching for weapons, though none of the beings made a move. Jake looked to the group and held up a hand, indicating to all not to make any aggressive moves, but to remain calm and relaxed.

Ralos continued.

"*There is no need for fear. We were here before the first stone was laid. We watched the gold seekers come, and we watched them die. We guided the last of the People to this refuge when the world burned around them. Now, you arrive. But not by chance".*

Jake whispered to Evelyn.

"Is this déjà vu or what?"

"Yes, I thought the same. He may not be Noah, but he is just as tall," Evelyn replied.

Dunmore's brother muttered under his breath.

"What the hell *is* this?"

Jake shook his head.

"Something way older than *we* ever guessed".

The alien - if that's what it truly was - gestured for them to follow.

As they walked deeper into the city, guided by both the ancient tribe and the tall ones, they passed murals that told an impossible story: a tale of ships descending from the sky, of a pact between the stars and the earthbound, of knowledge exchanged for sanctuary. Symbols on the walls began to shimmer as if reacting to their presence.

One mural depicted Conquistadors attempting to steal a black stone, only to be struck down by beams of light.

Another showed the same stone held aloft by one of the tall beings as the jungle grew around them like a living cloak.

Jake whispered to Evelyn.

"That stone you took from the chief...it's not just a relic...it might be a key to something here".

Evelyn nodded slowly.

"Yes, and I think we've just unlocked the gate to something far bigger than treasure".

The group followed their guides - half tribal, half something far older - through the winding stone streets beneath the jungle canopy. Vines coiled like veins across ancient walls, but nothing was ruined. Every structure stood firm. The air was cooler here, laced with a faint metallic tang, and though the city was cloaked in green, it felt as if the jungle obeyed its presence rather than the other way around.

At the centre stood a great circular plaza, and in it, a stone monolith covered in writing no one could recognise - except Mateo.

He froze, staring up at the engravings. His mouth parted slightly, and he stepped forward, as if in a trance.

Jake narrowed his eyes.

"Mateo...are you alright, mate?"

Mateo didn't answer at first. Then softly replied, "I have seen this before".

Evelyn turned to him sharply.

"Where?"

Mateo touched the carvings.

"My grandfather. He had drawings. He kept them locked away, like they were dangerous. He said our ancestors came from somewhere that was not just Spain. That our bloodline had...'star-blood.' I thought it was a myth...storytelling".

Lecky sighed and pointed to their hosts..

"Mateo, are you saying you're connected to *them*?"

One of the tall beings stepped forward, placing a hand on the monolith. The air shimmered again, and their collective thoughts heard the voice once more:

"His blood remembers. He is of the Second Root. Not born here, but born from those we entrusted".

"Entrusted?" asked Jake.

Everyone looked at Mateo.

Evelyn whispered.

"They left something behind...in your people".

Mateo backed away slightly, shaken.

"I do not know what they mean".

But the being only said, *"You will"*.

Then the stone monolith began to glow, and a seam split down its centre. A passage descended into the earth, revealing a spiral staircase carved with starlike patterns.

Ralos turned his gaze to Evelyn.

"The keys you took must return here. They open what should never have been closed".

Evelyn began to speak.

"But how...how do you know...?"

She slowly unzipped the side pocket of her pack and removed the black stones. They pulsed faintly in her palm. Ralos one reached out - not to take them, but to guide her forward.

Jake and Lecky glanced at Dunmore's brother, who looked uncharacteristically solemn now. His ex-special forces men stood ready but calm, as though they too understood they were now in something beyond worldly conflicts.

Lecky spoke quietly to Jake.

"We're not here to find gold anymore, are we?"

Jake shook his head.

"No. I don't think we are mate. I'm a bit confused right now, but stick with it".

Evelyn placed the two stones in her pocket, and, as she stepped down into the passage, stone lanterns lit on their own. Mateo followed...uncertain but drawn. The others moved after them, but before they could enter, the passage closed. They held their nerve and the city above remained quiet.

But deep in the mountains, miles behind, the Templars crept closer - drawn by the same pull, unaware of the force that waited within.

As the hidden passage sealed behind Evelyn and Mateo, the rest of the group was led deeper into the city by the remaining tall beings and members of the ancient tribe. The tribe, though human, bore distinct features that set them apart - tall, lean frames, angular faces, and eyes that glowed faintly in low light, like starlight reflected on still water.

Their language was melodic but peppered with strange, almost electric tones - words the tall beings understood with ease. Clearly, they had lived side by side for centuries. The relationship wasn't one of dominance or servitude, but quiet co-operation, as though the humans were caretakers of the surface, and the tall ones were guardians of deeper truths.

Dunmore watched them with rare curiosity, his usual smugness gone, tempered by awe.

"This...is not what I expected," he said, "they've quite obviously lived here for centuries...but they've built nothing new, just maintained and preserved it".

Jake nodded, eyes tracing the clean lines and seamless curves of the architecture.

"I reckon it's because they weren't meant to change it. They were meant to *guard* it".

Children of the tribe laughed as they darted through hanging vines and shallow pools. One girl tossed a glowing fruit up to Lecky, who caught it awkwardly and smiled, turning it in his hand. It smelled of cinnamon and citrus.

"Strange," he said, "but kind of peaceful".

Dunmore leaned in pessimistically.

"It won't *stay* peaceful. Not if your friends the Templars make it here".

Jake frowned.

"Then let's hope whatever's below us can stop that from happening".

Beneath the city, Evelyn and Mateo followed the glowing path of ancient lights, the black stone guiding them like a beacon. The staircase spiralled down for what felt like hours, the air growing thinner and colder the deeper they went. Strange symbols shifted along the walls - sometimes they seemed to be in motion, like they were alive, responding to their presence.

Eventually, they emerged into a vast underground chamber, circular, domed, and vast, like a tardis. Floating in the centre of the space was an orb of light the size of a house, suspended in mid-air by nothing at all. Around it were six stone platforms like petals, and a small obelisk on each, pulsing with energy.

Ralos turned to Evelyn.

"This is the Memory Core," he said, *"a record of what came before...before your history...before your stars had names".*

Mateo stepped forward slowly.

"Why bring us here?"

"Because, like the Spanish, those who now pursue you seek power. But they do not understand its purpose. They only want to steal our gold and to keep the truth hidden from mankind. We built this city not for conquest - but as a beginning".

The orb pulsed brighter.

Visions flickered inside - ships sailing between stars, ancient wars not of this earth, beings fleeing extinction, seeding knowledge into the bloodlines of early explorers, philosophers, prophets, conquistadors, even priests.

Evelyn's eyes widened.

It was more than a chamber. It was a vault of beginnings - the place where truth first touched the earth.

"This is where it all began".

Ralos nodded.

"And where it must be decided".

Suddenly, one of the obelisks flared red.

Far above them, the city trembled as a tremor rumbled. Jake and Lecky felt it. So did Dunmore's brother. The children stopped laughing.

Far off in the trees, a bird screamed and took flight - startled by something moving through the jungle.

Their pursuers were close.

The six obelisks encircling the glowing orb pulsed softly, like a heartbeat echoing through the chamber. Light shimmered from the orb in slow, rhythmic waves, casting the walls with glyphs that seemed to drift and breathe.

Ralos turned to Evelyn, his voice low and resonant.

"We came to your world long ago, seeking the Garden your kind calls Eden. We have searched many worlds, crossed galaxies. We were not the first to search for it, nor the last. But the signs here were unlike any other world - stronger, older. We believed that the Earth held the final path to it, but the last clues have always eluded us".

His eyes shimmered with something like sorrow.

"Eden is not a myth. It is real, a gateway between worlds. A cradle of life. But it is not merely of this Earth. It is a conduit - a place where creation touches its source. It is for those who walk in truth. It holds something older than memory - the essence of creation. The power it holds is not meant for one planet alone, and yet there are those who would steal its power".

Another figure stepped forward, silver-grey robes stirring as though caught in a wind none of them could feel.

"We are called the Arallim," it said, *"in your tongue, that would mean 'the Watchers of the Path.' We are not of this Earth. Our home lies beyond the Veil, far past the stars your kind has only just begun to map".*

Evelyn's breath caught, but she said nothing. The being continued.

"Long ago, we were like you - divided. Warring. Lost in the pursuit of dominion. But we were given a sign. A message woven into the very fabric of space and time. A calling. To walk the Way of Light, not conquest".

Mateo thought for a moment, paused, then spoke.

"A message from who senor?"

The being's eyes deepened, like staring into still water.

"From the One you call God. The Source. The Voice. The Light That Moves. He is not bound to one world or one people. He is the God of galaxies, of every soul that breathes".

"You believe in God?" Mateo asked, the surprise in his voice not hidden.

"We know Him," the being said simply, *"as the Creator"*.

Evelyn glanced toward the orb, her voice quiet.

"And you've been looking for Eden ever since?"

"We followed the echoes of His presence," said the first being, *"across countless systems. On many worlds, we were welcomed. On others, feared or hunted. Some tried to claim the message as theirs - shaping it into weapons, empires. But Earth...Earth was different. Here the resonance was stronger. This is the cradle"*.

Evelyn swallowed; overwhelmed. Then her eyes widened as a thought occurred to her.

"I might have something that can help," she said quietly.

She dug into her pack and pulled out a small, scuffed USB stick - so plain in its appearance, and yet, it might as well have been gold.

"We found the Garden of Eden almost two years ago," she said, her voice steady yet full of excitement. "We met the ones you'd know from our scriptures - Noah, Jesus...many others. They showed us what the world was meant to be through what is on this device...The Book of Truth. But when it came to actually getting it shared with all of humanity, we hit a wall. There are three physical copies, hidden. But I also made some digital versions. This is one of them".

She held out the USB.

"I figured the Crescent Templars wouldn't expect me to carry it into the jungle. So I did. If you've got a computer, I'd be happy to share it".

Ralos stepped forward, his gaze fixed on the tiny device. With great care - almost reverence - he accepted it, as though it were holy...which it was of course.

"We too searched for Eden for generations," he said softly, *"we never imagined it had been found...let alone by you. And this Book...we did not even know it existed...and you offer it freely?"*

"It's real," Evelyn nodded, "it talks about how we're all meant to live - every tribe, every nation, every world. In peace. In unity. It's not just history. It's a guide. It speaks to all of us. You can have the whole thing - it's yours".

Evelyn's mind suddenly drifted back to the black rock which she had taken from the chief days earlier and the one she had found at the ruined village. She reached into her pocket and took them out, offering them to the tall being.

"These...the keys that you spoke of...they belong here too, don't they?"

Ralos's expression changed - surprise, then deep relief. He froze, then stepped forward as she placed them in his palm.

"These are part of the Core," he breathed, *"a memory fragment. They were lost...long ago".*

He stepped to the central orb, where one of the stone obelisks had two hollow sockets recessed into its side. With hands that trembled just slightly, he inserted the black stones. The orb brightened instantly, casting dancing symbols across the chamber walls, some alien, some ancient, some somehow both. A deep, harmonious tone rang through the chamber, like a long-forgotten chord being struck again for the first time in ages.

He then took a pace back, emotion flickering across his features.

"Thank you," Ralos whispered, *"you have restored what we thought forgotten; re-awakened part of our history".*

Then, slowly, his gaze met Evelyn's and Mateo's, as he beckoned to them both with a large hand.

"Come," he said, his voice fuller now, as though carrying the echo of something greater behind it, *"we must feast...then, I too have a gift. For all mankind".*

Ralos led Evelyn and Mateo quietly up the spiral staircase toward the surface - the walls still vibrating softly behind them.

CHAPTER 11

THE GIFT

That evening, the city came alive with celebration.

Beneath the open sky, soft golden light spilled from strange, elegant stems that rose from the stone or arched overhead like branches. At first, they had looked like lanterns - but there was no fire, no oil, no wires. The light was cold and constant, humming faintly in the bones if you stood close enough. Jake had tapped one gently, half expecting it to flicker or spark, but it didn't even shudder.

"It's electricity," he whispered low to Evelyn, "but... not like anything we've seen. No obvious source...no wires...nothing".

Evelyn nodded.

"It's everywhere - even in the stone. It's powering the whole city...but how?"

They were still trying to work it all out. The beings around them - so human in form, but unmistakably not human - moved with grace and ease. Their expressions were kind, their eyes full of deep, knowing light. They still didn't speak aloud. Instead, they continued to touch minds gently, like a hand on the shoulder, warm and wordless. It was strange at first, but not uncomfortable.

Tables had been laid with strange and wondrous food - fruits that pulsed softly with colour, meats roasted over heatless flames, drinks that fizzed and glowed. Children darted past, laughing, chasing each other in spirals while musicians played instruments carved from bone and stone, their wild, rhythmic music vibrating in the air. The celebration was joyful, generous, and utterly alien.

Jake and Evelyn sat together on a smooth stone bench, hands intertwined. Neither said much - they didn't need to. Just being here, in the glow of it all, was overwhelming enough.

Even Lecky, usually full of questions, was slumped in a pile of cushions after sampling a blue fruit that had knocked him out for fifteen minutes. He had come to blinking and grinning, claiming he could see sound.

And still no one had shown them the gold or the mysterious power source.

"So I wonder what this gift is then?" Jake asked, watching the flickering lights above.

"I don't know, but maybe they're waiting for the right moment," Evelyn replied, "perhaps they don't trust us fully yet".

Jake grinned a silly grin and fluttered his eye lashes.

"How could anyone not trust this innocent face?"

Evelyn slapped him playfully on the arm.

"You silly bugger".

But not everyone was as patient.

Near the edge of the plaza, hidden in the shifting shadows behind a curving pillar, Alex and Richard Dunmore stood side by side, unsmiling.

Alex's eyes were sharp and restless.

"This is all a bloody distraction," he hissed under his breath. "Dancing. Fruit. Pretty lights. We didn't come all this way for a welcome party".

"They're hiding it," Richard said, "they've got something here. Something powerful. You can feel it".

"And if it's *that* powerful," Alex muttered, "then we're not leaving without it".

They watched as one of the taller beings moved through the crowd, stopping occasionally to rest a hand lightly on someone's shoulder - sharing a memory, perhaps, or a quiet reassurance. It never spoke, but people turned toward it with reverence.

"We need to find out where they're keeping it," Richard said, "tonight, while the others are distracted".

Alex nodded slowly, his eyes drifting to Jake and Evelyn, sitting close, oblivious.

At the centre of the plaza, the music changed - slower now, deeper. The lights dimmed slightly, shifting to an amber glow. From somewhere beneath their feet came a soft, resonant vibration. It felt...purposeful.

Several of the beings stepped forward, their attention turning toward the visitors. One of them tilted its head slightly - and Jake felt a gentle push at the edge of his thoughts.

A message.

"Come. It is time".

Jake glanced at Evelyn. She had heard it too. They both stood.

From the shadows, the Dunmore brothers straightened, watching closely.

Whatever this gift was - gold, power, or something else entirely - it was coming now.

Jake and Evelyn moved with the others as the beings guided them away from the feast, down a long, winding path flanked by the glowing stems of that strange light. The air had changed - still warm, still rich with the scent of spices and fruit - but quieter now. More focused. The kind of hush that came before something important.

Behind them, Alex and Richard Dunmore peeled off from the edge of the crowd, slipping into the darker gaps between the stone structures. They didn't follow directly - not yet. Instead, they circled wide, drawing their men in close.

The five men may have been hired muscle - armed, quiet, and obedient - but even *they* were beginning to shift uncomfortably. The atmosphere had unnerved them from the beginning, but now that they had seen the city in full, its scale and strangeness, its impossible lights and unspoken thoughts - it was getting under their skin.

"None of this feels right, sir. They're in our heads. I don't like it," said Mackie.

Alex shot him a look.

"Then keep them out. You're not here to *like* anything. You're here to follow orders".

The men glanced to Richard Dunmore, their *actual* employer, who just shrugged.

Mackie held his tongue, secretly wanting to break Alex's nose.

"Look around you," Alex said, "they've built a city above and below the ground that makes the modern world look primitive. They haven't aged. Their power - it's not human. And they're handing us a gift?"

Alex sneered and folded his arms, then glanced toward the procession of guests disappearing around the bend.

"No one gives away something like that for free," he said, "but they trust the scientists. They trust Evelyn and Jake. Not us. That's fine. Let them see the gift first - we'll step in when it matters".

But even as he said it, the men exchanged uneasy looks. The bravado was wearing thin. The deeper they went into the city, the more impossible it seemed. The light that didn't flicker, the walls that seemed to shift slightly when no one was looking, the music that could be felt through the skin more than heard with the ears.

The men found themselves glancing over their shoulders again and again, like something was watching - or waiting.

Still, none of them said anything more.

Not yet.

The path narrowed. The laughter and music of the feast faded behind them, replaced by a low, ever-present humming sound - the sound of something deep within the stone, steady and powerful. Jake tried to shake the feeling that it was alive.

Ralos and the other beings walked ahead, silent as always. No footsteps. No words. Just the occasional glance back - a subtle tilt of the head that was neither invitation nor warning, but something in between. Jake caught Evelyn's eye and saw the same unease there. She squeezed his hand but didn't speak. They couldn't speak - not in this place, not to their hosts. All they had were thoughts, impressions, feelings shared in brief flickers of understanding, and even *that* was growing less clear.

"It's like...they're holding something back," Jake whispered, "almost as if they want us to trust them completely before they show us anything".

Evelyn nodded.

"Or they want us far enough from the others before they reveal what the gift actually is".

Behind them, Tariq walked in silence, eyes darting from wall to wall. The lights were getting brighter - not lanterns, they now knew - but something else entirely. Soft globes fixed into the stone that cast no shadows, buzzed with energy, and never flickered. Lights that shouldn't exist in a city this old. Not without modern power. Not without something far more advanced.

Not far back, Richard and Alex's group had slowed. They were keeping their distance now, pretending to let Jake and the others lead - but it wasn't patience that held them back. It was caution. Richard's men had fallen mostly silent. Their earlier sharpness was dulling under the pressure of the city itself. Whatever confidence they had, whatever deal they had been promised, it was being replaced by something older...instinct.

A few of them shifted hands toward their rifles which were secured across their chests, not to fire, but for reassurance.

Alex noticed it and turned to his brother.

"They're losing their nerve," he whispered.

"They're smart," Richard replied, "which is a bit of a problem".

"They might be dangerous if they stop believing in us," said a worried Alex.

Richard's eyes followed the group ahead.

"Then we keep moving. We stay close. And when they show us where the power comes from, we make sure it ends up in the right hands".

Still, something in his tone had changed. Less confident. Less sure. The city was getting to all of them.

One of the men at the back stumbled slightly. Not from the terrain - the path was smooth - but from a strange sensation none of them could quite explain. Like something heavy had passed through him. He stopped, blinked hard, then shook it off as if it hadn't happened.

Jake heard the stumble and looked back at the five men.

"Drunk again eh boys?" he laughed, before whispering to Evelyn. "What are *they* doing? Something's going on with Richard's men. They don't look happy at all. And those two idiots are skulking in the shadows. They must think we are blind or something".

Lecky, who was a few paces behind Jake and Evelyn quietly spoke.

"I'm with you Jake. They are good guys yet the older Dunmore seems to think they will just obey him without question".

"Well, I think he will be in for a bit of a shock if he thinks soldiers are just bloody robots," replied Jake.

Lecky nodded his agreement as they kept walking, deeper into the unknown, each step slower than the last.

The corridor opened into a vast chamber, the ceiling arching high above like the inside of a hollow mountain. The structure was part temple, part engine - the ancient stonework entwined with vines glowing softly, pulsing with energy. Carved pillars lined the circular space, their surfaces engraved with strange runes and depictions of people from long ago: explorers in armour, wide-eyed conquistadors bowing before something magnificent.

The walls were smooth and seamless, etched with patterns that shimmered faintly beneath the strange electric light. The chamber glowed - not with torchlight, but with a strange, silent brilliance. It wasn't paint or metal - more like the stone itself had been changed, embedded with something living.

Beyond the pillars, inside the temple, piles of gold shimmered - coins, chalices, masks, jewellery. Mountains of it lined the walls in orderly ranks, filled great basins like molten sunlight turned to stone. But the treasure did not seem to be hoarded, and it certainly was not guarded. Simply resting, as though wealth meant little in this place.

Each member of the expedition stood frozen in the archway, faces lit by the golden glow. Not one reached for the stacks. Not even a whisper passed between them.

But the Dunmore brothers...they felt differently.

Alex's mouth curled into a grin.

"Now this," he breathed, "this makes it all worthwhile".

His older brother, Richard, stepped forward, his expression one of pure greed.

"Hundreds of millions," he whispered, "maybe more".

But what commanded the centre was something far greater.

Suspended in the air above a stone dais, a machine hovered. Spherical, made of smooth, interlocking metallic rings, it rotated slowly with an inner core that pulsed with shifting light - like a captured star. The sound it emitted wasn't mechanical but melodic, like a choir at the edge of hearing.

"This is the heart of our city," said Ralos, his words gently penetrating the minds of all present. *"A kinetic generator. It transforms motion into endless power. Clean. Eternal. A source of light, warmth, and life".*

Jake stared.

"No fuel? No emissions? Just... motion?"

"Yes," Ralos said, *"it was always meant to be shared - when your kind was ready to receive, not take".*

"Could it be used to power anything?" asked Evelyn.

Ralos nodded.

"It could be reduced in size to power the air machines we often see overhead".

"What about smaller craft that can be used on the ground?" Evelyn asked.

"Anything that you desire and can build can be powered by this," he replied.

All around were impressed. Finally the answer to the world's energy needs without damaging the planet.

"Can you show us how to build this?" enquired Jake.

One of the beings nodded.

Dunmore said nothing, but the gleam in his eyes was unmistakable. His brother wore the same look.

Jake saw it and muttered under his breath.

"Don't even think about it".

"What?" Dunmore said, feigning innocence, "I'm just admiring the engineering".

Lecky snorted.

"Yeah, like a magpie admires shiny things - just before he steals 'em".

But the Dunmore brothers' eyes weren't on the generator. They were fixed on the gold, each wearing the same calculating stare. The two stepped aside, conferring in low tones.

"This is it," Alex whispered, "forget the brotherly rivalry thing, let's unite and get rich".

"Really? And how are we going to do that?" replied Richard.

Alex thought for a brief second.

"We kill everyone, take the machine, fly it out piece by piece; and as for the gold, we'll be rich beyond anything we ever imagined".

Richard nodded.

"I'll issue the order. My men will follow".

He turned and shouted the command.

"Secure the exits. Wipe them all out. Leave no one alive".

But their hired guns didn't move.

The men exchanged glances, a feeling of unease rippling through their ranks. These were trained professionals, ex-military. Tough, yes - but not murderers. Not killers of unarmed children and adults.

Mackie stepped forward.

"Shove it up your arse you upper class twit," he said, "we signed up as security for a big pay day, not genocide".

"That's an order!" Richard shouted. "Do it!"

The men stood their ground, shoulders squared - defiant to the last.

Parks raised his left fist, then slowly mimed cranking an invisible handle with his right. With deliberate insolence, his middle finger rose like a flag.

"Wind that up, you bastard," he muttered.

Jake stepped forward.

"Stand down, all of you."

Richard gave a mocking snort.

"Don't be fools. Do you think your pay cheque is worth anything after this? You could buy a bloody island".

"We're not thieves," Jake said flatly, "we are guests here".

Richard's expression twisted.

"Then, you *are* a fool".

"We'll take it all," Alex said, as he turned - fast - drawing his sidearm, "*and* that generator. We might as well make the trip worthwhile".

"You're not serious?" Evelyn said, but there was no humour in her voice.

"Oh, we are *deadly* serious my dear," Alex sneered.

Richard raised his pistol too, and shouted at the men behind them.

"Grab what you can! Now!"

The five former soldiers didn't move.

There was a long pause. Then Mackie spoke again.

"We don't work for bloody pirates".

Richard's lip curled.

"Cowards!"

And then the atmosphere changed.

With sudden violence, Richard grabbed a nearby child - a small boy with shy eyes - and yanked him in front like a shield, jamming the muzzle of his pistol under the boy's chin.

Alex followed suit, seizing a girl no older than eight. She screamed, legs kicking, eyes full of terror.

As sudden as the threat of violence began, the chamber seemed to flinch.

A high-pitched whine sliced through the air, sharp and un-natural – like metal crying out. Sparks snapped from the base of the generator, scattering across the polished stone floor. The orbs spinning around its core stuttered in their rhythm, faltering like a heartbeat skipped.

Lights embedded in the walls dimmed and flickered.

The hum that had underpinned everything - that steady, calming thrum - cracked into silence.

Then a pulse. Low. Deep. Not sound, but feeling. A ripple of force that passed through every chest, as if the room itself had just drawn breath.

Evelyn froze, eyes darting to the generator.

"What the hell?"

Lecky took an unconscious step back.

"It's reacting. It knows".

The orbiting rings began to jitter, jerking like nerves under a surgeon's blade. Sparks arced again, brighter this time - licking at the air like lashes of warning.

The girl in Alex's grip screamed louder, her voice swallowed by the shriek of grinding force.

Jake raised his pistol slowly, never taking his eyes off Richard.

"Let the children go you gutless bastard".

Richard's hand trembled, but his grip on the boy stayed tight.

"Back off...or they're as good as dead".

The generator pulsed again, but harder this time. Dust rained from the ceiling like snow, and the lights flared blood-red.

The generator wailed.

And in that instant, every human instinct in the room agreed; the city had woken up.

The golden chamber erupted - not in action, but in panic. Mothers screamed in a language the team couldn't understand, hands reaching desperately, voices laced with fear. Fathers lunged forward only to be held back by the threat of being shot. The children, too shocked to cry, shook in their captors' arms, eyes wet, and faces pale.

Lecky caught Jake's eye. They didn't need to speak. Just a look. A slight nod.

Jake winked.

Lecky reached into one of the gold piles and casually plucked a coin free.

"Hey, Richard," he said, tossing it underhand across the chamber.

Richard's eyes flicked. Reflex took over.

He reached out to catch it.

Two shots rang out like hammer blows.

Jake's pistol was already smoking when Richard's body hit the floor, half his face gone. The gold coin dropped to the ground beside him and spun as if deciding in a game of chance.

Alex turned in shock - just in time for Jake's third shot to take him square in the temple. He dropped like a puppet with the strings cut, the girl tumbling safely to the floor beside him.

Silence.

Then a soft, wet sobbing as parents rushed forward to gather their children. The soldiers didn't move. Jake took a slow breath, his pistol still in hand, barrel pointed at the floor. Beside him, Lecky raised his eyebrows, gave a small approving nod, and winked.

"Nice shot," he whispered.

Jake didn't look away from the bodies.

"I wasn't aiming for style points, but yeah it wasn't too shabby eh?"

A heartbeat passed. Then Lecky stepped forward and picked up another shiny gold coin from a nearby stack and casually tossed it underarm at Richard Dunmore's corpse.

"Here...catch," he said dryly.

The coin landed with a dull ching on the stone beside the dead man's outstretched hand.

Jake let out a quiet snort.

"Too slow".

"Well," Lecky said, nudging one of the bodies with his boot, "I reckon that's one way to get out of profit-sharing".

One of the Richard's men gave a quiet chuckle, too tense to laugh properly.

Evelyn knelt beside the girl, brushing hair from her face. The child clung to her, her small hands fisted tightly in Evelyn's jacket, her whole body shaking with silent sobs. Evelyn whispered softly, not in words the girl could understand, but in tones of comfort - the universal language of care.

The girl's mother collapsed beside them, tears streaking her face. She cried out in her own tongue, her voice raw and trembling, clutching her daughter as if to anchor her to the world. Evelyn stepped back, giving them room, her own eyes welling with tears.

Nearby, the boy who had been grabbed stood frozen, his father kneeling beside him, speaking urgently, cupping the boy's face and checking for bruises. The boy didn't cry - not yet - but his wide, unblinking eyes told the story plainly. He had stared into the abyss and barely come back.

Jake holstered his pistol with a slow breath. Lecky moved to his side, watching the others tend to the shaken children and the stunned silence that had fallen over the chamber.

"You alright?" Lecky asked quietly.

"No," Jake replied, "but they are. That's what matters. And as for these two...they were warned".

Lecky breathed out sharply, then glanced down at the Dunmores' crumpled bodies, their bright red blood pooling on the smooth stone. The room had returned to stillness - but the shine on the walls seemed colder now.

"Well," he said with a shrug, "Pity. They might've lived longer if they hadn't been such greedy bastards. I guess they won't be needing that private island after all".

Jake gave a dry, mirthless chuckle.

"Yeah...I hope it's warm where they're headed".

Lecky laughed a knowing laugh.

"Well, after what we saw in Afghanistan I think *that* is a sure thing".

They turned back toward the group, where tension was beginning to give way to something like calm - fragile, but returning. The hostages had been pulled to safety, the parents clutching their children with trembling relief. A few of the tribesmen had begun to lower their weapons, whilst others simply stood in shock, staring at the lifeless Dunmores, as if unsure how the moment had truly ended.

Jake glanced again at the mountains of gold, the ancient power vibrating quietly in the walls, then back at the lifeless Dunmore brothers, crumpled on the floor like discarded refuse.

"*They* came looking for treasure and didn't care how they got it," he said.

Then, as the tension began to thin, eyes drifted again to the real prize in the room.

The generator.

It stood in the centre of the golden chamber, glowing softly. Elegant, alien - a construct of spinning rings and floating orbs, all orbiting a central shaft of radiant energy. No wires. No pipes. No controls.

And yet, impossibly, it thrummed with life.

Or rather...it had.

For a moment longer, it remained silent - dormant, like a beast testing the air after a storm.

Then, slowly, as if sensing the danger had passed, the lowest ring gave a single slow rotation. One of the floating orbs blinked - a pulse of light, then another.

The generator shuddered softly.

Its hum returned.

Not loud, but unmistakable. A deep, living rumble - like breath drawn in after being held too long.

The lights on the walls brightened in response, casting golden reflections across the chamber. The arcs of energy resumed their orbit, smoother now. Balanced. Peaceful.

Lecky let out a breath he hadn't realised he'd been holding.

"It's...alive again".

Evelyn stepped closer, eyes wide.

"I actually think it was afraid".

Jake looked surprised.

"Machines don't get afraid".

"Then it's not a machine," she said quietly.

Jake looked around at the walls, the strange warmth in the air, the way the floor almost seemed to vibrate in harmony with the generator.

"No," he said, "I get the feeling that it is something much more".

Ralos stepped forward, his silvery robe whispering against the stone floor. His voice reverberating through the minds of all present like a low chime in a vast cathedral.

"Did you too come to take the gold...or the power that sustains this place?"

The question hung in the air.

Evelyn stood still, her heart thudding. She met the alien's gaze - those deep black eyes indecipherable, ancient, and intelligent.

"No," she said, voice steady, "we came seeking answers...yes, maybe even treasure. But not to steal. We didn't know this city was still occupied - or that you watched over it".

She paused, then added with quiet honesty.

"What we found here is far beyond what we expected. We don't want to harm it. We want to understand".

Ralos studied her a moment longer, then turned to the others. His voice softened, though it still echoed.

"Many came before. They were greedy and reckless. They broke what they could not grasp...you did not".

A ripple passed through the tall ones, a silent exchange of thought or memory.

Then Ralos gestured toward the glowing machine at the heart of the chamber.

"Come. See what they sought to take. You make look closer. We will show you what they never earned".

The group hesitated only a moment before following.

The generator stood unchanged - floating, spinning, whispering in its quiet elegance. The orbs still danced around the shaft of light, casting reflections across the golden walls.

Evelyn approached slowly, a little hesitant.

Jake was impressed and gave a low whistle.

"They're letting us see it up close?"

Lecky grinned and nodded.

"Not just see it. I think they're offering more than that".

Ralos raised a hand. A shimmer passed through the air beside the generator, and suddenly a projection blinked to life - a cascade of glowing symbols and diagrams, rotating slowly in the space between them.

Blueprints. Schematics. Knowledge.

"We will give you the design," he said, *"to build, to learn, and to save this world".*

Evelyn's voice was barely a whisper.

"Why trust us?"

Ralos's gaze turned back to her.

"Because you did not touch until invited; and because you told the truth".

Jake glanced between them.

"So...we get a copy of the greatest power source ever built, just like that?"

Lecky elbowed him.

"Not just like that, buddy. I think we just passed the test".

The symbols continued to glow, spinning slowly; waiting.

"Do you have a device to store this knowledge?" Ralos enquired.

Evelyn reached in to her pack and produced a Tablet.

"I have this, but the battery has been flat for days," she said, "and I'm not sure that it will accept your superior technology".

Ralos beckoned her forward.

Evelyn reached out - not to touch the generator, but to accept the knowledge offered. A thin beam of light passed from the projection into the Tablet, which now sprang to life. The transfer was silent. Instant, and final.

The generator resumed its quiet rotation.

Behind them, the tall aliens stood still, watching not with suspicion, but with the cautious hope of those who had waited a long time for someone worthy.

The moment the data transfer ended, the projection faded. The chamber felt quieter somehow - not empty, but still. Watching. Waiting.

Evelyn looked down at the Tablet, now softly glowing with encoded knowledge beyond human science. Her hands trembled slightly.

Meanwhile the generator purred softly, its rings now turning with tranquil precision. Light pulsed again through the orbiting orbs, steady - no longer volatile.

She stepped closer, still holding the Tablet, her voice quiet. "Is it...alive?"

Ralos turned his gaze toward the generator. His expression, if it could be read at all, seemed thoughtful.

"No. It is not living. Not as you understand it. But it is responsive. It was created to sense imbalance...to detect violence, or the will to dominate. When it feels such intent...it ceases to function".

Jake exhaled sharply.

"So it shut down because of the Dunmores?"

"Yes".

Evelyn looked down at the Tablet in her hands, then up at the glowing machine.

"So if we take this knowledge back...if we build something like this...it won't work for just anyone?"

Ralos nodded.

"Correct. Only those without hunger for conquest will awaken it. It is not a weapon. It is a gift. And gifts are not given to the unworthy".

There was silence for a moment.

Then Lecky, of all people, muttered, "Well...that rules out about half of all governments then doesn't it?"

Evelyn didn't smile. She looked instead to Jake, to the others, and finally back to the alien.

"Then we'll have to make sure it's used by people who deserve it. People with good intentions".

Ralos inclined his head, slowly.

"That is the only way it will ever work".

Jake folded his arms, watching the rings revolve.

"So this isn't just a power source. It's a test of honesty and goodness".

"It always was," Ralos replied.

Lecky pondered for a moment before speaking.

"Hey, so that means that if we powered any sort of motorised vehicle with it then it could not be operated by anyone who wanted to commit a crime or anything like that?"

Ralos nodded.

"Wow...so no getaway cars, no tanks...no wars".

"I think this will be about as popular as the Book of Truth," laughed Jake.

"Huh...not if we don't tell anyone," replied Evelyn.

Jake winked in response.

The lights on the generator pulsed once, almost like a heartbeat - then settled back into rhythm, steady and alive.

Evelyn was still in awe of what she now possessed.

"I can't believe they just gave us this," she whispered, "it's...it is everything".

Jake didn't smile. He looked toward the aliens, his eye brows raised.

"So...why now? Why us?"

Ralos spoke again. His voice was calm, but something in his tone carried weight - memory, perhaps. Or a warning.

"Because you listened. Because you asked. Because you did not assume dominion".

Lecky thought for a moment.

"And the others?"

A pause. Then the alien answered.

"They came with greed in their hearts. They saw gold and wanted it for power. They saw the generator and, although they did not understand it, imagined themselves as gods".

Evelyn's eyes widened.

"Are you saying that this isn't the only generator?"

"That is correct".

The chamber fell silent.

Jake muttered, "Bloody hell".

Ralos gestured to the room.

"The gold is our currency. It was never the treasure. But the machine became a test of sorts".

Lecky gave a low whistle.

"And most people...failed?"

"All but you".

Evelyn swallowed.

"And the Dunmores?"

The alien tilted its head towards her.

"They failed the test before they ever saw the machine".

Lecky scratched at his temple.

"So...what do we do with this? We've got the plans for a miracle. What if we build it and *we're* not ready?"

The alien inclined its head.

"You are ready, but you must choose your friends wisely".

Evelyn blinked.

"What?"

Jake looked at Evelyn, then back at the aliens.

"Then I suppose we'd better get it right then".

"Do you mind if we take a closer look?" asked Evelyn.

The aliens said nothing but gestured towards the generator. As they stepped back into the shadows ringing the chamber, the softly glowing walls brightened a little - not just with light, but something like approval.

"Well, it's still running," Lecky said, stepping closer, "didn't even hiccup".

Jake narrowed his eyes into a squint.

"No guards, no shields, no warnings. Just sitting here, in the open".

Evelyn joined him, brushing her hair behind her ears as she studied the device.

"Maybe it doesn't need protecting. Maybe no one here would dare touch it".

"Perhaps all it takes is good old fashioned manners," Jake replied.

"Yeah, well," muttered Mackie, "two blokes just tried, and now they're on the floor".

Lecky laughed and looked towards Jake.

"Yeah but I think Jake deserves the credit for that one".

Jake glanced at the gold, then back at the generator.

"This city's running on something we don't yet understand. Power that shouldn't exist here - and technology that sure as hell isn't human".

Lecky crouched beside the machine, peering at the orbiting orbs, whilst scratching his chin.

"To think that this could power a city. Maybe more. The lights, the heat, the systems - all of it".

"Without noise. Without fuel. Without anyone even noticing," Evelyn added, her voice quiet with awe.

Jake looked around at the softly glowing walls and gently vibrating stone.

"Everyone thought the gold was the treasure," he said, "but this...this is the real reason people came...even if a few hundred years ago they didn't realise it".

Evelyn crouched near the generator, careful not to touch it. The rings still rotated silently, suspended in ways that defied gravity and logic. Each orb pulsed faintly - not with light, but with...presence. Like they were watching.

Jake knelt beside her.

"You know what this reminds me of?"

She glanced sideways.

"Don't say a meat pie in a microwave".

Jake playfully nudged her.

"You know me so well, but, seriously it looks more like the inside of a jet engine...if the jet was built by ghosts and ran on moonlight".

She smirked, but her expression turned thoughtful.

"There's no interface. No switches. No cables. It's not pulling from a source we can see - it *is* the source".

"I'm sure once we check out the plans all will be revealed," added Jake.

Lecky hovered a few steps back, arms folded, watching like a wary parent at a science fair.

"Tell me it won't blow up if someone sneezes".

Jake snorted.

"Mate, if this thing could blow up, we'd already be vapour. It's not unstable. It's...patient".

"Or self-aware," said Evelyn.

That earned a look from Jake.

"Hang on...so we've gone from Indiana Jones to the Terminator? Bloody hell".

Lecky scratched his chin.

"She's not wrong," he said, "you feel it too, don't you? Like it's...alive".

"Nope," Jake said, flatly, "I feel like its glowing and not plugged in. And that's weird enough".

Evelyn hesitated. Then she turned to the aliens still watching from the chamber edge.

"Well, it sort of is".

Jake whistled low again and 'gazed around the chamber.

"So not only is it the power source, it's the bouncer too? I'm just waiting for Arnie to suddenly appear in a flash of light".

Lecky gave him a look.

"This isn't a pub, or the movies, Jake".

Jake leaned back on his heels and looked at the others.

"Yeah, yeah, but I just fancied saying 'I want your clothes, your boots and your motor cycle'. Anyway if this *is* powering the city, maybe even other cities…what's keeping it going?"

Evelyn hesitated.

"It's not nuclear. It's not solar. No heat signature, no decay. I mean, obviously it is kinetic, but what kick started it in the first place?"

"Magic?" Lecky offered, half-joking.

Evelyn raised an eyebrow.

"Or physics we haven't earned the right to understand yet".

"Well I suppose once we get back home and build one, all will be revealed," replied Jake.

CHAPTER 12

DANGER CLOSE

That evening, the city came alive with celebration.

Beneath the open sky, platforms shimmered with hanging lanterns of crystal and living light - glowing softly, pulsing in rhythm with the music. Tables groaned under the weight of unfamiliar fruits, roast meats sizzling on open flames, and drinks that sparkled like fireflies in glass. The air was rich with the scent of spice and smoke.

Children danced in spirals, trailing ribbons and laughter. Musicians played instruments carved from bone, and translucent wood, their wild melodies echoing through the trees. The tall ones clapped and stamped their feet, their joy unburdened by the centuries they'd spent in hiding.

Mateo found himself pulled into a circle dance by two tall warriors and a tiny, barefooted girl who refused to let go of his hand. Her eyes sparkled, and she grinned each time he stumbled. Lecky bit into a bulbous purple fruit, sighed with pleasure - and promptly passed out briefly, under a table.

When he regained consciousness, he claimed he had seen a donkey made of honey, and went back for seconds.

Evelyn and Jake sat quietly, hand in hand, watching it all, both too overwhelmed to speak - but not needing to. Tariq smoked something passed to him by a laughing elder and began reciting what may have been poetry, though it came out in a bizarre mix of Pashto and English.

The celebration stretched long into the night - not just a feast, but a rite of trust. A promise shared without words.

"You are welcome here".

At dawn, with gold light threading through the canopy, Ralos summoned them once more to the temple.

The chamber felt different now - no longer solemn, but sacred in another way. A place where something had changed.

"You have given us hope," Ralos said, his voice like stone worn smooth by time, *"and for that, we have another gift for you"*.

He gestured to a pile of gleaming gold coins, and other artefacts shaped like leaves, suns and stars.

"Each of you may take a share - equal to the weight of a new-born piglet. No more, no less. We offer it not as payment...but as a gesture of peace".

Tariq looked to Evelyn as he recalled the crystal mine in Afghanistan which had made them both multi millionaires, and gave her a silent nod. She said nothing, but smiled faintly.

Lecky clapped his hands.

"Well that settles it - I want the fattest piglet in the whole jungle; preferably one that's been overeating for weeks".

A ripple of laughter moved through the group.

Jake smiled, but his thoughts were firmly on the plans which had been downloaded onto Evelyn's Tablet the previous day; clean, limitless energy. The kind of technology that could save the world...or be the death of them.

"The gold is fine," he said, "but the plans...they change everything."

Evelyn nodded as she patted her back pack.

"If we're wise enough to use them right".

Ralos stepped forward then, eyes darker now.

"We have walked among your kind for millennia," he said, "before your cities, before your borders. We have watched your rise. And your falls. In the deep forests. Beneath your oceans. Inside your mountains. Always waiting".

"Waiting for what?" Evelyn asked.

Ralos raised his hand.

"For someone to listen. For a generation whose first instinct is not fear. For humans who would not greet us with guns".

The words settled heavy in the space between them.

"*We tried once,*" he said, "*to meet you openly. In the time your history calls the Nineteen Fifties. One of our vessels fell in a place you call...Roswell*".

Jake felt a chill.

"Area 51? That was real?"

Ralos nodded once.

"*Very. Your soldiers came quickly. Not to help, but to seize. They killed the survivors. Dismantled the ship. Hid the evidence. Then told lies so loud no one could hear the truth beneath them*".

Evelyn looked down.

"I believe you".

"*Not all humans are like them,*" the alien said, "*some ask instead of accuse. Some reach out, even when they are afraid. You are the first we have met who listened*".

He looked at them each in turn. Jake, Evelyn, Tariq, Mateo, Lecky and Dunmore's five men.

"*You did not try to control. Or steal. Or conquer. You came with open eyes*".

Jake nodded slowly.

"And we'll protect what we've been given. I give you my word".

Lecky raised a hand.

"Quick question - do I still get the fruit? I'm kind of hoping for a second donkey".

Jake interrupted.

"Sorry everyone but I think our friend here is still a little tipsy from last night".

Ralos smiled faintly.

"*You may take as many donkeys as you wish, Lecky*".

Lecky gave a contented sigh.

"Best alien encounter ever".

Jake looked out at the waking city, the glow of the lights fading into morning light, and then at his companions.

"Let's not be the people they were hiding from".

"Let's not," Evelyn agreed.

Above them, the canopy swayed - as if the whole city was listening.

The farewell feast had stretched long into the night - firelight dancing off gold-veined pillars, drums echoing through the trees, and the scent of roast meats and sweet jungle fruits lingering in the air. Evelyn and the others had danced alongside their hosts, laughed, and tried - poorly - to mimic ancient steps passed down through generations.

Now, the atmosphere had turned reverent.

The city elders and their alien brethren stood by the stone path that led back into the jungle, draped in flowing robes stitched with luminous thread. Ralos stepped forward and pressed a leather-wrapped bundle into Evelyn's hands – a physical copy of the kinetic generator blueprints.

"You came in search of a myth," he said. *"You leave with a seed".*

Evelyn bowed her head.

"We won't waste it, I promise".

Another of the tall beings raised a small wooden scale.

"And this," he said with a smile, *"is your weight in gold - measured against the piglet of your choosing".*

Laughter followed at the thought of Lecky's earlier comments, and each team member gently hefted a squealing piglet while the city's youth brought coins of ancient gold, polished to a warm gleam. The moment was light - even surreal – but evil lurked somewhere in the tree line.

The morning air was heavy with mist, the jungle beyond the city walls quiet but watchful.

Jake shouldered his pack - now heavier with the gold coins gifted to them - and looked one last time at the gleaming city, its crystal domes and spires catching the early light like shards of sun.

Evelyn stood beside him, brushing hair from her face.

"We have been so lucky. I just hope we can do their gift justice".

"I reckon with the wealth it will bring us we can not only save the world but maybe even help those who are less fortunate than us," Jake replied.

Evelyn smiled and planted a kiss on Jake's lips.

"My husband the benefactor..."

Jake stared into her eyes.

"Husband? But I haven't even proposed yet," he replied as he dropped down on one knee.

Evelyn's face beamed with love as she reached out to pull Jake back to his feet.

"I think I already have".

"Well you always were a woman of the world...when shall we do it?" Jake asked.

"As soon as we can...but somewhere warm," replied Evelyn.

Jake hugged her tightly.

"You're on mate...the sooner the better".

Lecky exhaled, oblivious to Evelyn and Jake's engagement.

"I still say I should've picked the fattest piglet".

The alien beings and the city elders, robed in silver and gold, offered no words of farewell - only solemn nods. A pair of warriors walked with them to the edge of the jungle, then vanished soundlessly into the green.

Behind them, the five ex-soldiers moved tactically - eyes sweeping, weapons ready. Jake was the lead scout, Lecky close behind. The sky above was streaked with rose gold, the jungle quiet, almost too quiet.

They had made it a mile down the path when the peace shattered.

A sharp whine sliced through the air.

Explosions echoed, sharp and unnatural. Birds scattered. Somewhere, a monkey screamed. Then - bullets tore into the undergrowth.

One of Dunmore's men was hit in the leg; his comrade returned fire and dragged him to cover. Evelyn screamed uncharacteristically as a round struck a tree inches from her head. Jake tackled her to the ground, his weapon bouncing into the ferns.

"Ambush!" Lecky shouted, diving behind a fallen log.

"No shit, Sherlock!" Jake yelled back.

There were too many shadows. Too many guns.

From the forest edge came the attackers - Templars. Clad in red and black, their insignia gleamed: a silver crescent piercing a blood-red cross. Their boots pounded like war drums.

And leading them, flanked by riflemen, stepped Father Benedict - robes torn, eyes fanatical, a crucifix in one hand and a pistol in the other.

"You walk with heretics and demons," he sneered, "but your steps end here".

Three of the ex-soldiers opened fire, dropping two of the Templars - but the rest moved with brutal precision, overwhelming them, cutting them down in seconds.

Jake lunged for his rifle - but a boot pinned his hand to the earth. Benedict loomed overhead.

"You don't deserve the Book," the priest spat, raising his weapon, "and now you'll *never* deliver it".

Everything went black.

Jake awoke to the blare of street lights and the roar of a crowd.

They were back inside the city – bodies bruised, faces bloodied, dragged before the temple steps. The remaining Templars - maybe fifteen now, likely summoned by radio or satellite phone - stood guard, weapons raised at the silent crowd.

Benedict stood triumphant, pistol in one hand, Evelyn's backpack in the other.

"Give us the true Book!" he barked, holding the bag aloft, "or we raze this cursed place and salt the soil!"

The beings said nothing. Then a young warrior stepped forward.

He did not speak.

He raised his arm.

From the rooftops and alleyways, the city rose.

Warriors with crystal-tipped spears and blades made from living bone surged forward with inhuman speed. Arrows streaked through the air, glowing as they flew. Templar rifles cracked - two warriors fell - but the others moved like wind through streets.

Jake grabbed a fallen pistol and rolled behind a stone pillar whilst Lecky kicked a Templar in the knee and took his rifle. Evelyn looked around at the distracted Templars, took her chance, and elbowed one of them in the throat and dived for cover.

The square exploded into chaos - muzzle flashes, smoke, screams. Alien weapons sliced through body armour with impossible ease. But the Templars were more prepared than expected; a helicopter suddenly appearing above, lowering as if to fire.

Ralos raised one hand.

From the jungle, a searing lance of blue-white light shot up, struck the aircraft dead centre, and ripped it apart in mid air. The wreckage vanished into the trees.

One Templar tried to throw a grenade - but a warrior pushed him into a well before it exploded.

Benedict roared like a madman, bloodied and wild-eyed. He seized Evelyn by the arm and yanked her in front of him, jamming the barrel of his pistol to her temple.

"Come any closer and she dies!" he bellowed, backing toward the temple steps.

Evelyn struggled, elbowing him hard in the ribs.

"Let go of me, you arsehole!"

Jake didn't hesitate. He charged straight at them, boots pounding across the broken ground.

"Let go of her you gutless bastard!"

Benedict swung the pistol toward Jake. Evelyn took her chance and threw a wild punch - but Benedict ducked, and her fist smacked Jake square in the jaw.

"Bloody hell, Evie!" Jake grunted, staggering sideways, "if you wanted me out of the way you could have just said so!"

The moment's distraction was enough. Jake launched himself, tackling Benedict around the waist. The three of them crashed to the ground in a tangle of limbs. The pistol went off with a deafening crack - too close - but the shot flew wide.

They wrestled in the dust. Evelyn scrambled clear as Jake slammed his forearm across Benedict's throat. Benedict bit, clawed, and tried to bring the gun around again, but Jake locked his wrist and twisted.

"You're finished mate!" Jake growled through clenched teeth.

He finally got the upper hand and with a vicious wrench, Jake ripped the pistol from Benedict's grasp and rolled free. One breath, two - then he fired.

The shot echoed off the temple walls.

Benedict went limp. His crucifix clattered on the stones. His final breath came not in prayer, but with a look of stunned confusion - as if he had finally realised who the true heretics were.

Jake sat up slowly, rubbing his bruised jaw and looking over at Evelyn with a half-smirk.

"Next time you punch someone, try aiming for the lunatic with the gun, not the bloke trying to save you".

Evelyn stepped over, brushing dirt from her shirt with mock delicacy.

"Well, next time don't block my line of fire".

When the last Templar fell, silence returned. Smoke curled. Blood soaked the flagstones.

No one cheered.

The city stood still, proud - as if it had never moved.

Then Mackie muttered, "We've got trouble".

On the horizon: helicopters. Three of them. Fast. Black. Coming low.

"They must've called for reinforcements," Lecky panted.

Ralos approached, calm.

"You must go. Now," he said. *"They will not stop".*

Lecky clutched his side - blood on his shirt, but still standing. "What about you?"

Ralos smiled faintly.

"We are not without teeth".

He raised his staff, and a stone wall at the base of the temple slid open with a groan of grinding rock.

From the shadows emerged tall alien figures - silent, luminous-eyed. Hands raised in readiness. They had stayed hidden - until now.

"Follow the serpent path," Ralos instructed, *"it will take you beneath the city - to the edge of the jungle".*

Jake nodded.

"Thank you. For everything".

He helped Evelyn to her feet, whilst each of them retrieved their packs and weapons. Tariq nodded once in silent gratitude.

"They will follow," Ralos warned, *"not all are dead. Go".*

Tariq swore under his breath - rare for him.

"Then let's keep moving," Jake said grimly. "We've come too far to die in a bloody tunnel".

Ralos laid a hand briefly on Evelyn's shoulder.

"Whatever happens - the truth and the power must survive".

The remaining seven friends slipped into the dark passage as the door began to close behind them. Just before it sealed, a hiss of movement - four Templars slipped in behind, unseen.

And then - silence.

Above, the helicopters began to descend.

And the old city readied for war.

The tunnel twisted like its namesake - narrow, wet, pulsing with old heat. The walls shimmered faintly, lit by Jake's torch. Behind them, the door had sealed. Ahead: only silence.

They moved in a line - Jake first, rifle raised. Evelyn at his side with a curved blade she had taken in the battle. Tariq followed with grim focus, gun in hand. Lecky, Mackie and Parks brought up the rear with Mateo, who still clutched his pack of gold like a child refusing to part with his toys.

"Where are we going?" Mateo whispered.

"Out," Tariq muttered. "Hopefully".

"And the Templars?" Evelyn asked.

Jake didn't answer.

He didn't need to.

Behind them came a soft clatter. A boot on stone. Four shadows. Armed. Hunting.

They picked up speed. The air grew colder, the tunnel tighter. They crouched low, hands scraping mossy walls.

Then - a junction.

Two paths.

Jake hesitated.

"Split up?"

"No," Mackie snapped. "They'll pick us off".

"I could leave the gold here," Mateo offered. "Maybe it will tempt them?"

"No," Lecky said. "You earned it. But we might use it differently".

He reached into his pack and flicked two coins - one down each tunnel.

Clink. Clink. Clink.

Silence.

Then - voices. Spanish. Low and tense.

Two went left. Two went right.

Jake grinned grimly.

"Nice work".

He pulled aside a broken mosaic and revealed a narrow crawl way - a hidden third path. Ralos must have meant for them to see it. They slipped inside one by one.

And behind them, the hunt continued.

But for the first time, they had a lead.

Time lost all meaning. The dim tunnels twisted endlessly, a suffocating maze of stone and shadow. They moved in tense silence, weapons ready, boots stirring ancient dust. Only the drip of water and the rasp of their breath filled the dark.

Then - distant gunfire. A startled shot. A scream.

A Templar. Off course. Ambushed.

The aliens must have joined them in the tunnel.

Jake raised a fist - too late. They stumbled into a chamber.

Circular. Colossal. Timeworn stone walls enclosed a yawning pit at its centre. Four narrow stone bridges stretched from edge to edge, crossing like spokes on a wheel.

Jake cursed under his breath.

"Trap written all over it".

A shout behind them - boots pounding.

The last three Templars stormed into the room, guns raised. No words. Just cold fury.

Crack...!

A bullet ricocheted off the stone near Evelyn's head, flinging chips into her hair.

Jake spun, fired - caught one in the thigh. The man shrieked, staggered, and pitched into the pit, limbs flailing into the void.

"One!" Jake shouted, already moving.

Evelyn darted right, luring one across the far bridge. Her blade flashed in the gloom. The Templar followed, snarling, a combat knife gleaming in his fist.

Jake and Tariq split left, drawing the second one. Parks and Mackie hugged the edge of the chamber, weapons up but holding fire, eyes tracking every move.

Mateo dropped behind a pillar, hugging his gold like a child's teddy bear, wide-eyed and shaking.

Gunfire cracked again. Jake staggered, a fresh burn slicing across his shoulder.

"Bollocks!" he hissed, teeth gritted.

Tariq lunged - tackled the Templar mid-span. They crashed to the stone bridge, fists hammering, elbows cracking bone. The Templar twisted, slammed an elbow into Tariq's ribs, and reached for his pistol...

Mackie didn't hesitate.

"Oy!"

With a grunt, he hurled his pack.

A full kilogram of gold caught the Templar square in the face with a sickening *crack*. The man reeled, arms waving like a mad man, and tumbled off the bridge into the pit with a fading scream.

Mackie's pack skidded after him – teetering on the edge.

"No, no, no...!"

Mackie launched himself forward with the desperation of a man saving a child. He landed hard, arms outstretched, and snatched the pack just as it tipped over. His boots scraped dangerously close to the edge, pebbles clattering into the abyss.

He lay there for a second, hugging the loot to his chest.

Then, breathless, he spoke.

"Bloody hell. That was nearly the most expensive throw of my life".

Parks and Tariq helped haul him back.

"You always were a bit of a tosser buddy," joked Parks.

Mackie just grinned and kissed the bag.

"She's fine. We're both fine".

"One left!" Evelyn called, voice taut with focus.

All eyes turned.

Evelyn and the final Templar circled each other on the outer rim of the chamber, on the farthest bridge. Their blades flashed in the dim light, metal kissing stone and steel with each clash.

He was strong. Brutal. Trained to kill.

But Evelyn danced like flame - not faster, but smarter.

The Templar lunged, feinting high.

Evelyn ducked under his swing and twisted behind him, slashing at his thigh - not to kill, but to drive him back. She glanced down, eyes narrowing.

A cracked tile.

She faked a stumble.

The Templar grinned - stepped forward.

The tile crumbled.

His foot plunged through.

"No...!"

The bridge split with a groan, stone giving way. The Templar tumbled with a shriek, vanishing into the black.

Silence fell. Just the ragged sound of breathing and the distant drip of water.

Evelyn stood alone, chest heaving, blade low.

Mackie whistled.

"Remind me not to piss her off".

Jake chuckled, holding his bleeding shoulder.

"You and me both".

Parks stepped forward, offering Evelyn a canteen.

"Nicely done ma'am. Clean. Efficient".

Evelyn accepted it, took a swig, then tossed her hair back with a breathless grin.

"Well," she said dryly, "I thought I'd give you boys a show".

Jake limped over, smirking.

"Next time, warn me when you're planning to go all Zorro on us".

She gave him a once-over, then smiled.

"Perhaps next time, try not to get shot while I'm working".

"Believe me I hope there isn't a bloody next time mate," replied Jake.

Mateo peeked out from behind the pillar, still clutching his loot.

"Are we...done?"

Jake exhaled slowly, wiping blood from his temple.

"Yes mate...well I hope so anyway".

They moved across the remaining bridge, each step cautious, wary of more traps. The tunnel ahead sloped gently upward. Wind whispered through.

A shimmer of daylight winked at the far end.

Freedom - or the next nightmare. But at least, they were together.

As they stepped out into the humid jungle, the tunnel sealing behind them with a dull *grind*, Evelyn looked at the others.

"All that death," she said, "for a book".

Jake shook his head.

"More like for the fear of it".

In the distance, thick black smoke coiled into the sky - the last traces of the chaos they had left behind. The battle in the city was over. Every helicopter lay twisted and burning on cracked stone plazas. No rescue was coming. No pursuit.

Lecky checked his bag. Still heavy. Still clinking.

"I'm starting to think gold's not worth the trouble," he muttered.

Mackie clutched his sack tighter.

"Speak for yourself mate".

They turned toward the distant mountains.

Behind them, the canopy was eerily still. No rotors. No gunfire. No city.

Just a wall of green, swallowing secrets whole.

CHAPTER 13

HERE WE GO AGAIN!

They left the hidden city behind. No going back.

The mountain range loomed ahead - dark spines cutting across the horizon, cloaked in mist and storm-brewed clouds. The rainforest lay beyond, but it would take days to reach it. They would have to cross every obstacle again: the cliffs, the canyons, rickety bridges, the skeletal remains of an old jungle temple. And now they were fewer.

No one spoke of the three men who had died in the clearing, cut down by Templar fire, or the Dunmore brothers, but their ghosts walked silently behind them.

Jake led the way through the steep switchbacks, leaning into the steep inclines and trying to stop gravity pulling him speedily to the bottom of any downward slopes. His face was hollowed by fatigue, dirt caked in the lines around his eyes. Evelyn kept close, scanning the compass, then the skies, then the undergrowth, never trusting that they were safe. Jake limped but said nothing, having sprained his ankle in the earlier fight. His shoulder was burning too from the bullet wound, but he soldiered on..."no pain no gain" the army PTIs had told him many times during his career.

Lecky helped where he could, but even he was slowing, his earlier graze and bruising now taking its toll.

"I must be getting too old for this," he thought to himself.

It rained on the second day - a sudden torrent that turned the red trail to mud and forced them to shelter in the hollow of a cliff wall. That night, they slept restlessly, clutching their weapons and gold alike. Thunder echoed through the peaks like ancient drums. Somewhere, an animal howled.

"Oh pipe down will yer!" Parks called out.

By the fourth day, the jungle began to rise again on the far side of the mountains - green, steaming, endless. The canopy was thick, the air heavy. Jake recognized a gnarled tree twisted by lightning.

"We're close I think," he said.

The jungle was humid with heat and silence. Gone was the distant hum of the city's life - no chants, no drums, no glimmer of gold. Only vines and leaves, birdcalls, and the squelch of boots through mossy ground.

They walked in silence. Until Evelyn paused.

"Something's wrong".

Jake stopped.

"What?"

"Listen".

They did. And for a moment, all of them froze.

No birds. No monkeys. No insects. Just the whisper of wind and...footsteps.

Tariq whispered, "I do not think we are alone".

He was right. Figures began to emerge from the green. One, two...ten. Silent. Painted in red ochre and ash, masked in bone and clay, their weapons drawn.

"Here we go again!" exclaimed Lecky.

Jake looked around at the others and signalled for them to lower their weapons.

"Hang on a sec...I think we should play the game for a moment and see what goes on".

"Oh for Pete's sake put it down," Parks said to Mateo, who was clutching the gold-laden bag like a newborn.

Mateo hesitated, then dropped it with a clink.

A tall warrior stepped forward, obsidian-tipped spear gleaming. He gestured to the ground.

"I think he wants us to kneel," said Evelyn.

"Now *that* doesn't sound good," said Lecky.

Jake did as requested. The others followed.

The warriors closed in, close enough that their breath stank of fire and sweat. One pressed a spear to Jake's chest. Another hovered a blade near Evelyn's throat.

Then - a cracked voice broke through the ring. An elder stepped forward. He spoke in Spanish.

"You have returned from the city?"

Jake looked to Evelyn, who nodded.

"Yes".

"You were not expected to live".

Jake was frustrated.

"What's he saying?"

"He says he didn't think we'd leave the city alive," replied Eve.

Jake laughed.

"Yeah, we're full of surprises eh?"

"You entered sacred land. Walked paths forbidden to outsiders".

The elder stepped closer.

"But the chief who led us - he was cruel. He went after you. He never returned".

Both Evelyn and Mateo translated for the others.

There was a beat of silence.

"You brought justice," the elder said.

They didn't understand at first.

But then spears lowered. Bows relaxed.

"You may go," the elder said. "With our thanks".

Evelyn blinked.

"What?"

Mateo was overjoyed as he translated the elder's words.

Jake stood.

"We're...free to leave?"

"You brought change," the old man said. "Now we begin again".

Mateo bent to pick up his bag.

"Gracias," he said. "For not murdering us".

A few of the warriors even smiled.

They passed through the circle in silence.

Mackie whispered to Jake.

"So we're heroes now?"

Jake shook his head.

"No mate...just survivors".

Lecky, bringing up the rear, grunted.

"Best kind of heroes though".

They walked on.

Behind them, the jungle swallowed everything.

The jungle path opened before them again. No longer hostile. No longer entirely familiar. As they moved on, green engulfing them once more, laughter - small, unsure - began to creep back into their words.

Jake wiped his brow.

"So...next trip?"

"Somewhere with plumbing," Lecky said.

"Somewhere with bars," added Parks.

Mateo held up his bag.

"A bank in which to deposit this".

They all laughed, despite the ache in their legs, the stink in their clothes, the shadows behind them.

Ahead, somewhere through the trees, the battered Land Rover waited. And with it, the first real road home.

It was exactly where they'd left it - half-swallowed by vines, covered in leaves, and leaning slightly to one side like it had grown tired waiting for them.

"Still here," Lecky remarked, "like a loyal dog".

Jake pushed aside the foliage.

"Or a rusted coffin".

Parks popped the bonnet, poked at the engine, then gave a satisfied nod.

"She'll be fine I reckon".

Evelyn flopped into the passenger seat.

"Just for once I'd like an expedition to end with a hot shower and not a tetanus shot".

Mateo hauled his gold-stuffed bag into the back.

"You say that now senorita, but this little lady is about to take us straight to my first party as a rich man".

"And don't forget that this *was* your idea," Jake added.

The Land Rover roared to life - just barely - and after a judder and a cloud of black smoke, they rolled back down the rutted track toward the edge of the jungle.

The Hostal hadn't changed. Same stucco walls, same squeaky ceiling fan in the lobby, and the same old jukebox by the bar that only played two songs without skipping. One was a weepy ballad, the other a manic polka. Neither was welcome, but both were inevitable.

But tonight, the old place was alive. Full to bursting with dusty backpackers, and locals drawn in by the smell of grilled meat, cheap rum, and the kind of laughter that only comes after surviving something no one can explain.

Mateo stood awkwardly atop a table in the centre of the room, his face red from the heat and the attention. His shirt hung open, sweat-stuck to his chest, and in his hand - held aloft - was a single gold coin.

"To curses that did not kill us!" he called out, his voice cracking just slightly at the end.

A roar of approval rose from the crowd, followed by a shout from Mackie.

"To not turning into frogs!"

Another bottle clinked. Firecrackers went off somewhere outside. Laughter, smoke, and stories filled the gaps between.

Mateo grinned shyly as he hopped off the table, only to be immediately slapped on the back by someone twice his size. He took it with a startled chuckle and ducked back toward the bar.

Evelyn was already there, leaning on the counter with a cold drink pressed to her temple. She reached into her bag and pulled out a wad of folded bank notes, neatly counted. She placed them gently into Mateo's hands as he approached.

"I told you I'd pay you," she said. "Guide rate. Plus danger bonus".

Mateo's eyes went wide.

"Senorita, this is...too much...I have the gold. That is plenty enough".

"You walked through hell with us. And you didn't run...take it...you earned it a thousand times over".

He stared at the money like it might vanish, then quickly tucked it into his shirt with a grateful nod.

"Gracias. I will help my mother. Maybe fix the roof".

Jake passed by, catching the end of it.

"And maybe buy a new shirt while you're at it".

Mateo gave a sheepish grin and looked down at his sweat-stained, half-buttoned mess.

"Sí. That too".

At the far table, Lecky leaned back with his boot propped on a chair, sipping from a chipped glass.

"You realise that kid's gonna be mayor in a year. Or dead from a hangover".

"I'm betting mayor," Jake said.

"To dead mayors everywhere," slurred Mackie from the shadows, raising his own drink.

Laughter rippled again, and someone tried to make the jukebox play something decent. It failed. The fan overhead squealed like it was protesting about the noise of the party.

Out on the balcony, the warm night buzzed with insects and distant animal calls. Jake leaned on the railing, letting the noise fall behind him. Evelyn joined him, a second drink in her hand, this one untouched.

He didn't say anything. Just listened.

"So," she asked after a while, "what now?"

He considered it. The jungle had taken their energy, their clean clothes, and three good men. It had given back gold, nightmares, and something harder to explain.

"No story," he said finally, "not one that we can tell anyway".

"Not if we want that city to remain hidden that is," replied Evelyn. "Then we have the generator".

Jake smiled faintly.

"Yeah. Sell the power, keep the lights on. Big, honest money".

"And the rest?"

He glanced over his shoulder. Mateo was trying to teach a group of English girls how to flip a coin across their knuckles, failing miserably, whilst Tariq and Lecky were arguing about whether or not the parrot on the wall behind the bar had always been stuffed.

"The rest," Jake said, "we forget. Or guard. Like they did".

Evelyn sipped her drink.

"Not much difference".

"No," he agreed. "But we made it back".

Jake stared out into the humid night, the muffled laughter from inside drifting through the open shutters. The sky above was dark velvet, the stars blurred by jungle haze.

Evelyn moved closer, now standing beside him, smiling, her shoulder brushing his, and slipped her fingers into his rough hand.

"And then maybe a wedding," she said softly. "Somewhere quiet...Mediterranean coast?"

Jake raised an eyebrow.

"With real plumbing and definitely no ancient death cults?"

She smiled.

"That's the dream".

He squeezed her hand.

"Alright. But if anyone shows up with a spear or speaks in riddles, I'm leggin' it".

Evelyn leaned her head against his shoulder.

"That's a deal. But only if we can find a lovely church and venue somewhere".

He laughed; a deep, worn-out sound.

"We survived a cursed city, Evie. I'm sure we can survive wedding planning".

Behind them, someone popped another firecracker and the jukebox skipped and played half a verse of the polka before dying completely. No one noticed.

Jake didn't even flinch.

The rickety twin-prop plane banked low as it began its descent. Below them, the runway lights of Philip S.W. Goldson International Airport twinkled against the darkening landscape of Belize. The wheels squealed as they kissed the tarmac, and for a moment, it felt like the plane might fall apart around them - but then the skidding evened out, and the engine sputtered into a steady grumble; Evelyn took a deep breath.

They were back.

Jake looked out the window and there, just beyond the airstrip fence, sat Dunmore's sleek private jet - engines cold, door sealed. A ghost.

"I can't believe that thing's still here," Evelyn said, adjusting her bag on her lap.

Lecky peered through the window.

"Fitting. Let it rot here. Like the rest of his lies".

The heat hit like a wall as they stepped out of the twin-prop plane. The same pilot from their inbound trip, a sharply dressed Englishman, stood waiting, his arms folded, jaw tight, a silk cravat wilting against his neck. His polished shoes gleamed, despite the dust, and he looked very much like a man who had spent the last few weeks brooding in a climate and country he considered beneath him.

Jake barely had time to approach before the man snapped.

"Where the hell have you been? And where is Lord Dunmore?"

Jake didn't miss a beat.

"Indisposed".

The pilot narrowed his eyes.

"I was given very specific instructions to wait here. I have been *baking* in this damned swamp for weeks".

"I'm sure he'd want you to be compensated," Jake said, pulling out a thick wad of cash and tucking it into the pilot's blazer pocket, "consider this overtime...and a new flight plan".

The Englishman glanced down at the cash protruding from his pocket, visibly recalculating his mood.

"Where to?"

"London," Jake replied.

The four friends laughed - wearily, warily, but honestly. It felt strange, touching down in the world again. There were no temples here, no golden spears, no aliens in cloaks; just sweat, dust, and fuel fumes.

Before they left the Hostal, they had said their goodbyes.

Mateo, still bashful even with money in his pocket and half the bar chanting his name, had hugged Evelyn awkwardly and promised to visit Europe - "when I get a passport..."

Mackie and Parks had gone their own ways too - both richer, both changed. Mackie had taken off at dawn, muttering something about Panama, a yacht, and never trusting museums again. Parks, oddly sentimental, had shaken Jake's hand and said he might finally retire - or start a podcast, or both. Both had grins like men who had outrun a curse.

By the time they had refuelled, grabbed bottled water, and loaded their gear, Lecky stood apart from the others, watching a taxi pull up.

"I've got a contact in Houston," he said. "Old friend who owes me a favour. I'll be fine from here".

Jake stepped forward and shook his hand.

"Thanks mate. You were solid and stuck with us all the way".

Lecky chuckled.

"I'm not built for tunnels or temples. But I know when I've seen something bigger than myself...twice now in fact".

He held up one of his gold coins.

"There's a beach house somewhere with my name on it".

Tariq shook his hand firmly whilst Evelyn gave him a quick hug.

"Be safe, Lecky".

"You too...and hey..." he pointed at them with a grin, "next time someone hands you an ancient map or a journal...burn it".

Jake grinned.

"We'll see you again for sure...you'll see".

"You won't," Lecky said with mock sternness, "unless you find Atlantis".

"Now there's an idea," said Evelyn.

"Don't even think about it," laughed Jake.

They watched as the taxi disappeared out of sight.

Then the pilot shouted from the door of the jet.

"Are we leaving or what?"

Jake smiled.

"I think we'll 'what'," he said, offering his hand to Evelyn, "do you want to 'what' with me?"

Evelyn took his hand.

"Let's go home".

The three climbed aboard. The door sealed. The engines roared to life.

Inside the cabin, Evelyn dropped into a plush seat and exhaled, whilst Jake gazed out the window, watching the Belize night blur past the glass. The jet began to taxi. Its nose lifted. The runway fell away. And as Belize slipped away beneath them, they didn't look back.

Not this time.

The Gulfstream G800 private jet banked gently over the endless blue of the Caribbean. Islands dotted the water like scattered emeralds, and white clouds cast slow-moving shadows on the ocean below. Inside the rattling fuselage, the three friends sat in relative quiet - exhausted, relieved, and contemplative.

Evelyn leaned back with her hat tipped over her face, but she wasn't asleep.

"You know," she said, her voice muffled by the brim, "somewhere down there - just off the Turks and Caicos - they say Captain Kidd buried a chest of gold. Real gold. Pirate gold. That's if you believe in such things".

Jake arched an eyebrow.

"After what we've just been through, I believe in everything".

Evelyn smirked, nestling against Jake's shoulder.

"Not everything. Just the useful bits".

Tariq gave a tired laugh.

"We have plenty of gold and other riches do we not? Let us agree not to go chasing ghosts for at least another year...yes?"

"No promises," Evelyn said, curling an arm around Jake, "though the idea of pirate treasure does have a certain appeal".

Jake opened his eyes and stroked his chin, then looked at them both - sunburned, scratched, and one kilogram of pure gold each richer.

"I'm out, mates. London's calling. A quiet life, maybe some holidays abroad, you know relaxing on a beach somewhere - just as long as nothing tries to kill me of course".

"Yeah right," laughed Evelyn.

Jake turned to Evelyn, his fingers brushing hers.

"Don't you ever get tired of treasure hunting and stuff?"

"Not really," she said, "especially when there's a whole world of secrets still buried out there".

Tariq chuckled from across the aisle.

"It does not appear that this lady shares your opinion about a quiet retirement".

Jake and Evelyn shared a look - the kind that held promises.

"No...that's a bit of a bugger isn't it mate?" Jake replied.

"Hah!" Evelyn laughed, ""you love it really".

"It comes with loving you I suppose," replied Jake as he closed his eyes and resumed his nap.

Somewhere in the distance, thunder rumbled over the sea. Or maybe it was cannon fire, echoing from a long-lost wreck beneath the waves.

The plane lifted again, climbing toward London.

Adventure, it seemed, was not quite done with them yet.

CHAPTER 14

TO THE FUTURE
AND BEYOND

Rain ran in silver lines down the windows of Evelyn's office, blurring the city beyond into a grey smudge. The radiator clicked and hissed. An old iron fireplace sat cold in the corner, beneath shelves crowded with books and files. The room smelled of ink, paper, and the sharp tang of rain-soaked wool. It felt safe - but it wasn't.

Evelyn stood at the window, her arms folded, watching the weather. Jake sat on the leather couch, elbows on his knees, hands steepled. Across from him, Tariq perched stiffly on the edge of a chair, shoes wet from the street. Between them, their three copies of the *Book of Truth* lay closed on Evelyn's desk. Silent. Ancient. Waiting.

"We're done with the companies," Jake said.

He spoke quietly, but his words hit the air like dropped stone.

"Every single one wanted the same thing - rights, patents, royalties. Not one of them asked what the world needed. Just what it could pay".

Evelyn didn't turn.

"It was never going to be different".

Jake looked at her.

"You hoped".

She gave a humourless smile.

"No. I just wanted to see their faces when they turned down salvation".

Tariq cleared his throat.

"They do not see it as salvation. They see...opportunity". His accent rolled the words out slowly. "Gold, not light".

"And they'll kill to own it," Jake said, pointing towards the desk, "same as the Book".

At that, Evelyn turned from the window. She walked to her desk and placed a hand on the cover of one of the books. The leather was warm under her touch, as if the thing were alive.

"It was never lost," she said softly, "it was hidden. Eden didn't bury it. It waited...and now we can do something about it".

Jake stood.

"We publish it then. The whole bloody thing; *and* in every language".

Evelyn nodded.

"I for one am sick of these politicians and so called religious leaders. We let the world read the truth".

"Just to show our sincerity, and that we mean business, all profits should go to charity," Jake said, "every penny".

Tariq gave a small nod.

"Yes...I agree...clean water...education...food".

"Let them say it's a hoax," Evelyn said, "they will. But it won't matter. It'll be out for all to see and judge for themselves".

Jake looked at her.

"We do interviews?"

"Every camera we can find," she said. "TV, podcast, web, radio. Let them see us - and let them know we're not afraid".

Tariq rose from his chair. He moved to the desk and touched the brief case that held the generator plans.

"And this? What do we do with this?"

"We keep it safe along with the digital copies and share it with no-one," Jake said.

"Then how do we build it?" Evelyn asked.

Jake walked to the bookshelf and pulled a pen from a mug. He held it up.

"One part at a time. We split the design into pieces and find a few local engineering factories who want to make loads of money in the future; people who don't ask too many questions but know how to make machine parts. Each business gets a section and no one sees the full design. I reckon once we have the individual parts we can assemble it ourselves...it looks pretty straight forward".

"No one but us eh?" Evelyn said.

"Exactly".

Tariq's dark eyes glinted.

"They build, but do not understand. They *see*, but they are blind".

Jake nodded.

"We assemble it in sections. Somewhere off-grid. Quiet. No headlines".

Evelyn glanced at the window. The rain had eased, but the sky remained bruised. Her mind drifted back to *The Book of Truth*.

"They'll come for us again".

"The Crescent Templars?" Jake said. "I don't think so...not once the book is published. With the book and the generator, the church, governments, even private industry...everyone who profits from silence will hate the noise we're about to make".

Tariq smiled thinly.

"Then we must make it loud my friends".

Silence settled. Outside, a siren wailed in the street below - the everyday kind. But it reminded them all of what was coming.

Jake walked to the Book and opened it. The words shimmered - just for him. Just for now.

"We start tomorrow then," he said, "no more waiting. We go *very* loud".

And in the stillness of that quiet London office, something shifted - something that hadn't moved in centuries. As if the world had just drawn breath.

The studio lights were hot. Jake shifted slightly in his chair. He hated suits - the collar always felt like it was strangling him. Beside him, Evelyn looked composed, regal almost. Her makeup was perfect, but her eyes were steel. She wasn't here for a chat. This was war.

The interviewer smiled, all teeth and polish.

"We're joined tonight by Doctor Evelyn Kane and Mister Jake Allsop, whose discovery in the Middle East has already sparked controversy across the globe".

Camera One lit up.

The interviewer leaned in.

"Doctor Kane, let's begin with the book. You're calling it...the Book of Truth?"

"Yes...well not *us* exactly...the title was already chosen," Evelyn said, voice calm, "it predates the Torah, the Bible, the Qur'an...in fact all scriptures. It speaks of Eden - not as myth, but memory – of the true word of God. It was hidden, not lost. And now it's here".

"And you're publishing it?"

"*Have* published it," replied Evelyn.

Jake nodded as he held up a copy.

"Every word. Worldwide. No redactions. It belongs to everyone".

"Some say it's a fake. Others say it's blasphemy".

"Good," Jake said, smiling, "if everyone's angry, we're probably on the right track".

The interviewer blinked, then turned to Evelyn.

"And the money?"

"Money?" she asked, surprised.

234 - TONY SQUIRE

"Yes...surely this a stunt to make you all rich?"

"A stunt?"

Evelyn was shocked at the sinicism from the interviewer.

"*All* profits," she said, "*every* penny from book sales goes to charity, helping science and communities. No governments. No religious groups. No middlemen".

Jake raised his hand like an excited schoolboy then quickly snatched it down.

"And don't forget small local assistance too...you know...new kit for kids' football teams...that sort of thing".

The interviewer ignored Jake.

"And the technology you claim to have found - the generator?"

Evelyn paused, then glanced at Jake.

"We're building it," Jake said. "Ourselves".

"Why not sell the design?"

Jake's eyes narrowed.

"We offered. They wanted to own it, bury it, or turn it into profit. So we walked".

Evelyn added, "The large prototype will power a town. But we're also building smaller units - ones that can power a car, a single house. Quiet. Clean. Safe. No power grid or petrol, and no more bills".

The host blinked again.

"You're serious?"

Jake leaned forward.

"We're beyond serious mate...this is the new industrial revolution...JET Kinetics Limited is in business".

The light on Camera One faded. The segment ended.

Backstage, Tariq waited, arms folded, too shy to go before the cameras. He grinned as they approached.

"You speak well," he said, his accent rich and lilting, "but now the wolves have heard you".

"Let them come," Jake said.

Six Months Later – Disused Airfield, Kent – Media Demonstration

The clouds parted just as the rust-red Mini rolled out from an old RAF hangar. Cameras flashed, drones buzzed, and reporters jostled behind ropes for a clear view. A dozen were live-streaming. The buzz had been relentless for weeks.

Jake and Tariq stood next to the car, whilst Evelyn, poised and professional, addressed the press.

"This is *not* electric," she began. "There's no battery, no fuel tank, no solar panel. What you're about to witness is kinetic generation - the first of its kind".

She gestured to the car.

"For those of you who know your cars, this is a 1968 Mini Cooper. The petrol engine, exhaust, and fuel system have been stripped out. In their place - our smallest generator yet, custom-built to power the vehicle using only motion".

Jake stepped into the car, nodded to Tariq, and turned the key.

No roar. No chug. Just a soft hum as the vehicle moved. The car rolled forward, picked up speed, then looped around the field, weaving past traffic cones. No exhaust. No noise. No hesitation.

As it stopped, Jake climbed out and opened the bonnet. Inside: a sleek black core, no larger than a microwave.

"*This* powers the car," he said. "It stores and reuses every ounce of energy. Braking, vibration, even potholes. No more petrol. No more charging. Just drive".

A stunned silence followed. Then came the thunder of applause.

Tariq grinned from the sidelines.

"They were not ready," he said under his breath, "but now they *must* be".

A Few Weeks Later – Tuscany, Italy

The applause had long faded, the buzz long since shifted to headlines and speculation. But here, in the hills of Tuscany, there was only peace.

A television sat quietly in the corner of the old villa's sunroom. The windows were thrown open to let in the evening air. Beyond them, vineyards rippled like a green sea, the sky warming to gold.

Jake sat on the edge of a deep armchair, shirt sleeves rolled up, his glass of wine untouched. Evelyn stood behind him, her hands resting gently on his shoulders, watching the screen.

Tariq entered with two espressos, handing one to Evelyn, then leaned against the wall beside the fireplace, arms folded. He said nothing, just nodded toward the television.

The news anchor spoke in crisp tones over slow-cut footage.

"JET Kinetics Ltd," she said, "is now officially the most valuable company on the planet".

Behind her, images rolled like a dream, towns in Kenya, Nepal, and Bolivia - their streets glowing gently beneath rows of lights powered by kinetic electricity stations. Families cooking, hospitals open through the night for the first time.

"In just six months, this trio have revolutionised global energy. Their patented kinetic generators now power homes, vehicles, farms, and factories. With much of their profits still going overwhelmingly to charities, the public has dubbed them...*The Barmy Billionaires*".

The screen showed the three of them on the factory floor, arms linked, smiles worn and honest, not rehearsed. Behind them: the banner, bold and simple.

JET Kinetics – Power for the People.

Jake squinted at the screen, then cracked a grin.

"We should put that on a T-shirt".

Evelyn smiled, her fingers tracing idle circles on his shoulder.

"You'd wear it to the wedding if I let you".

Tariq chuckled softly from the fireplace.

"Do not give him ideas".

Outside, cicadas buzzed in the olive trees. The wedding was in three days. A dozen guests were already scattered throughout the villa and its grounds. But for now, it was just the three of them, and Tariq's family, again - no press, no boardrooms, no noise.

Just the hum of something they'd built together.

The hills of Tuscany woke to birdsong and honeyed light, and by mid-morning the villa grounds shimmered in white and gold. Rows of chairs lined the olive grove, petals scattered along the aisle between them. The scent of olive and lemon trees drifted through the warm air.

Jake stood beneath an arch woven with vines and white roses, fingers tugging slightly at his collar. Tariq, standing beside him, gave a barely perceptible nod - steady as ever. The guests hushed as a string quartet began to play.

Then came the crunch of footsteps on gravel.

Evelyn appeared at the top of the aisle, sunlight catching the lace of her dress like frost on morning grass. She wasn't clinging to Lecky's arm - she never would - but she walked with him at her side, chin proud, eyes locked on Jake.

Lecky, scrubbed up and out of uniform for the first time in years, leaned in and whispered something that made her laugh. Probably something about not tripping over her dress. Jake didn't care. He couldn't stop smiling.

When she reached him, Lecky gave her hand to Jake with a gruff nod, then stepped back without a word.

The ceremony was short. Evelyn wouldn't have it any other way.

When the vows were done and the kiss stolen - slow, sweet, lingering - a cheer rolled through the grove. Glasses clinked, musicians struck up a lively tune, and the sun poured down as laughter and stories flowed like the wine.

They danced barefoot in the dust. Jake led clumsily, and Evelyn whispered corrections, laughing. Tariq, along with Miriam and their two young children, was dragged into a folk circle by a gaggle of aunts. Lecky gave an impromptu speech about loyalty and friendship, and only choked once. No one mentioned money, or factories, or kinetic power. Just love, and luck, and how the world had changed.

Later that night, the moon rose silver over the hills, and lanterns flickered across the courtyard.

The next morning came gently.

Jake sat shirtless on the edge of the bed, tea steaming in one hand, the white sheets a tangled mess behind him. Evelyn, still in one of his shirts, was perched on the window ledge, legs tucked up, watching the sunrise.

"Well that was a night to remember," Jake said.

Evelyn laughed.

"You'd better believe it big boy..."

Jake paused for a moment, trying to suppress a smile.

"Quiet out there," he said, taking a sip of his tea.

"Mmm...especially back home," she agreed. "Managers have the factories under control. Nothing to worry about really".

Jake smiled.

"Aye...finally a quiet life".

Evelyn turned her head, one brow cocked.

"I wouldn't go that far...pack your bags".

"What?"

He blinked, looked at her, then out at the sunlit horizon, and let out a laugh.

"Do I at least get to know where we're heading for?"

She slid down from the ledge, padded over, and took the tea from his hand.

"We're going hunting for pirate treasure".

He stared at her in disbelief.

"The Caribbean," she said, already pulling out a battered map from under a pile of wedding cards. The parchment was old, the ink faded, and a red X marked something just off the coast of a forgotten island.

Jake took one look at it and shook his head.

"You *really* are serious..."

She wiggled both eyebrows in the classic Groucho Marx fashion, holding the expression just long enough to make him laugh.

Jake sighed.

"This isn't about Captain Kidd's treasure, is it?"

Evelyn held out her hands as if waiting to be hand cuffed, leaned in, a wicked grin on her face, kissed his cheek, and whispered:

"It's a fair cop...but I'll come quietly".

Jake laughed inside as his thoughts turned to the previous few hours.

"That'll make a change!"

Originally from England, Tony Squire is now an Australian citizen, residing with his wife Sheila. A former soldier, since 2019 he has been writing books for both children and adults, bringing history to life through engaging characters and narratives. His works for younger readers introduce imaginative and adventurous tales, through his characters Buckley the Yowie, and Little Timmy, while his historical novels for adults explore the remarkable stories of the ANZACs during the Great War. More recently he has ventured into the world of archaeological thrillers, following the adventures of Evelyn Kane as she uncovers long-buried secrets and navigates dangerous landscapes in pursuit of the truth.

More Books By This Author

The ANZAC Chronicles:

"UNTIL YOU ARE SAFE..."
"TO OUR LAST MAN"
"OUR LAST SHILLING"

The Evelyn Kane Mysteries:

ESCAPE TO EDEN

Other Titles:

IN THE COMPANY OF OUTLAWS - MY LIFE WITH
NED KELLY AND HIS GANG